P9-DFD-363

Unforgivable

"Is there anything
you'd find — unforgivable?"
"I don't know." He grinned.
"I mean, if someone got *killed*,
yeah, I guess —
how come it seems
like I'm not answering
this right?"

Also by
ELLEN EMERSON WHITE

White House Autumn
The President's Daughter
Friends for Life
Romance Is a Wonderful Thing

point

LIFE WITHOUT FRIENDS

Ellen Emerson White

SCHOLASTIC INC.
New York Toronto London Auckland Sydney

*For my sister, Sarah,
who has been a lot of help
over the years*

ISBN 0-590-33829-3

12 11 10 9 8 7 6 5 4 3 2 1   12   8 9/8 0 1 2 3/9

Chapter
One

The way her father slammed the car door made Beverly's ears hurt.

"Inside," he said, teeth gritted.

Her stepmother walked in-between them, either keeping them apart, or physically trying not to take sides. Not that she wasn't on Beverly's father's side. Everyone was.

Mrs. Montgomery, who was baby-sitting for Oliver, opened the apartment door for them. She had probably been standing at the window for the last two hours. The kind of woman who would really get a thrill out of baby-sitting for Professor Johnson while he took his daughter to court. Beverly could just hear her on the phone to half of Greater Boston: "Poor Dr. Johnson. His reputation's just ruined. Had to take that girl of his — you know, the one who's been in all the trouble? — to the trial for that drug case. She's trouble; t–r–o–u–b–l–e; trouble. He wouldn't have custody at all, but the mother kilt herself, don't you know."

Slowly, Beverly unbuttoned her raincoat. Her stomach was hurting terribly and she wanted to go take some Tagamet, but her father was bound to make a pronouncement and she'd better wait for it.

He was waiting too, waiting for her stepmother to pay Mrs. Montgomery, who was being quiet, but taking her time getting her coat and pocketbook, obviously dying to hear some gory details.

"Thank you very much," Beverly's stepmother said, smiling at her. "I'll stop over tomorrow morning, and you can give me a list of whatever groceries you need."

That was an exit line and, reluctantly, Mrs. Montgomery left. She would probably die of curiosity before she got halfway across the street. Unless she had a glass in that big black pocketbook and was going to hold it against the door to eavesdrop.

Her father looked at her, and Beverly could almost hear him grinding his teeth. A habit both of them had. Some mornings, her jaw would hurt so much that it would be hard to open her mouth. Nice to know that she had periodontal disease to look forward to.

"For starters, Beverly," he said, his voice very tight, "you're going to — "

"Nick, why don't you go sit down?" her stepmother, Maryanne, suggested. "I'll run up and check on Oliver, and then I'll bring you a drink."

He frowned at her, frowned harder at Beverly. "Go up to your room," he said. "I don't want to see you for a while."

Beverly went, not looking at either of them. Halfway up the stairs, she felt a wave of such incredible nausea that she had to lean against the banister. The nausea faded back to ordinary pain and she continued to her room, closing the door. She thought about crying, but her stomach hurt too much and she went out to the bathroom to get her medication. The hall was empty, and she made it back to her room without her father or stepmother accosting her.

Avoid stress situations, her doctor had said last year when he first diagnosed the ulcer. Situations like murder trials? Yeah, murder trials would probably count. The ulcer had never made sense to her. You weren't supposed to be sixteen — seventeen now — and have a stupid ulcer. It sure did hurt like hell though.

She lowered herself onto the bed, lying as flat as she could, inhaling slowly, deeply. Sometimes deep breaths helped. Sometimes.

A *murder* trial. Well, actually, it was a hearing. She had never been so terrified in her life — no wonder her stomach felt this way. Tim had given his best performance: all blond and muscular and clean-cut, too wholesome to have possibly committed murder. Except that he had. Twice. And from the way he kept smiling over at her, the malicious smile that scared her even in the safety of a crowded courtroom, she knew that he wanted everyone to think that she was lying and had helped him every step of the way. And by knowing he had done it, and being too afraid to tell anyone, maybe she had.

There was a knock on the door, but she didn't answer. Her stepmother came in.

"How's the pain?" she asked.

Beverly sat up, moving her hand away from her stomach. "What makes you think I'm in pain?"

"Did you take your medicine?"

"Yeah."

"Good." Her stepmother put her hands in skirt pockets, looking very uncomfortable. Straight dark hair, dancer-thin, wide brown eyes. Young eyes. Today she was conservative in grey flannel, but ordinarily, she wore dramatic hippie sort of clothes — big wool ponchos, huge hoop earrings, black ballet slippers. And jeans. Always jeans. Not a person Beverly could take seriously as a mother figure.

"Is there anything you'd like to talk about?"

Not with you. Not with *anyone*. Beverly shook her head.

"Are you sure?"

Beverly nodded.

"He's more disappointed than angry."

Right. Beverly closed her eyes, willing the stomach pain to leave. "May I be alone, please?"

Her stepmother sighed. "If that's what you want."

Beverly nodded.

"I'll bring you some dinner later."

Beverly opened her eyes. "I'm not very hungry."

"Maybe you will be by then."

"No." Beverly shook her head. "Thank you."

Her stepmother moved closer. "Beverly, I — "

Beverly stiffened, not wanting to be touched, and her stepmother withdrew.

"I'll come back when dinner's ready," she said, and left the room.

Alone again, Beverly relaxed somewhat, letting her hands unclench. It was hard to believe that life could get any worse than this. More than once lately, she had thought about killing herself, erasing the fact that she had ever existed. It would be so easy, so — except that she wouldn't. She didn't respect people who committed suicide.

4

Chapter
Two

One night, when she was in the ninth grade, her mother didn't come home from work. She was half worried and half angry — it wouldn't be out of the ordinary for her mother to spend a little too much time at a bar after work, or even during work. She would have told her father, but after the divorce, he met some stupid graduate student at Harvard and they had ended up getting married, and Beverly *really* didn't want to live with him. Not that living with her mother was much better. Those last couple of years, it seemed like half the time, her mother was drunk, and the rest of the time, she was crying. Sometimes she did both at the same time. Beverly didn't know what to do, but was afraid to tell anyone because then she would have to go live with her father and his wife. She tried bringing home a couple of bad grades to give her mother something different to worry about, but her mother cried harder. So Beverly went back to getting A's. Also, getting dinner. Her mother wasn't eating much.

Then one night, right before Christmas, her mother didn't come home. It got to be eight, then nine, and Beverly was scared enough to call a woman who worked in her mother's office to ask if she had seen her. It turned out that her mother had never come back from lunch. Really scared now, Beverly was going to call her father, but then she saw red flashing lights outside.

An accident, the police said. There was a lot of talk — talk she probably wasn't supposed to hear — about blood alcohol levels and how fast the car was going — but the police called it an accident. Since when was it an accident to be thirty miles away from home on a mountain road going in the wrong direction and conveniently run into the largest tree around?

Her father drove up from Boston and brought her to the apartment where he, his new wife, and his new son lived. She didn't talk to anyone, not even the psychologist who was costing her father at least sixty dollars an hour.

She finished the ninth grade at a school in Boston, a terrible five months of sitting in the last row of classrooms, constantly afraid that she would cry, not making any friends. And then, in the tenth grade, she went to the Baldwin School in Cambridge. There were a couple of kids she knew from her old school, but she had managed to perfect a cool, distant attitude, and no one bothered her.

Since she didn't have anything else to do, she kept getting A's, and when her English teacher asked her to join the newspaper staff, she did as she was told, still not making friends. She even joined a couple of other activities, like yearbook, and chess, so her father and other people would stop worrying about her mental health and leave her alone. Sometimes, especially on the newspaper, someone like Colleen Spencer from her old school would say something funny or ask a friendly question, and she would want to relax, open up, but was either too afraid, or too much in the habit of being cool and distant. Everyone else seemed so cheerful and normal, like they all came from 2.3-children-BMW-families, and had never had anything bad happen in their lives. Oh, there were divorces all over the place, but that seemed more chic than traumatizing. It was easier to keep to herself.

Junior year, everything changed. Tim Connors started hanging around. Handsome, popular jock, even more bored and cynical than she was, he had probably been invited to every prom and cotillion in the Greater Boston area. Suddenly, he was paying attention to *her*. Appearing whenever she turned a corner, sitting with her at lunch, showing up at her locker. "We're just alike, Bev," he was always saying. "Neither of us gives a damn about anyone." "I give a damn about *you*," she would want to say, but Tim wasn't into emotionalism. And she fell completely, totally in love; was so happy that her father and Maryanne noticed and seemed to relax about her. Her father didn't quite approve of the boy who came swerving up to their brownstone in his Porsche, beeping the horn instead of coming in — although, the first time, her father had *insisted* on meeting him. Tim was the kind of cool guy who "didn't do" parents.

Now it all seemed incredibly stupid, but at the time, she had been convinced that he was wonderful. And he *was* charming. Because they never talked about families — his parents were never home and he had

the whole third floor of his house to himself, anyway —
and he never asked her how she felt about things, she
relaxed, knowing that she would never have the pressure of having to talk about her mother — or anything. So it was easy to give in to other kinds of
pressure: getting high, doing some coke, sex. He had
a lot of parties, and she found herself hanging around
with a bunch of jocks and their shallow girl friends
and genuinely enjoying herself. She *needed* to escape.

Besides, she was careful. She almost never got high
at school, she kept her grades up, she went to Planned
Parenthood and got the Pill. And if her father was
upset, or worried, or mad, it didn't seem all that serious, since she would be going off to college soon
enough. A year and a half wasn't *that* long. He never
actually caught her at anything anyway, just suspected
her. She was too careful to get caught.

When Tim started selling drugs, it didn't seem that
bad. He was careful, too — letting other people take
the risks, mostly just being a supplier. She wasn't really
sure where he got the drugs — somewhere in Boston — and she never asked, not wanting to know. No
one would ever suspect him: handsome, popular Tim
Connors, as All-American as they came. And because
he didn't seem to worry or care, she didn't either.

But he was becoming erratic — driving faster, taking more drugs. Then, one afternoon, with just the
two of them at his house, they had an argument. Her
father was having company for dinner and she knew
she shouldn't drink anything. Tim didn't like it, angry
enough to scare her. She tried to leave, but he blocked
her way, punching her when she tried to get past him.
She fell back against the wall, too stunned to react,
and he hit her several more times, yelling terrible

things, angrier than anyone she had ever seen. She didn't cry until he was finished, staring down at her, out of breath.

"Tell anyone about this and I'll *really* hurt you," he said, and ran.

She told her father and Maryanne that she had been mugged.

"Why did you lie?" the police had asked, later.

"I don't know," she'd told them. To protect herself? To protect him?

"Do you realize that if people had been aware of Mr. Connors' violence, Peter Mason and Colleen Spencer might still be alive?"

"Yes, sir," she'd said. "I guess I do."

That lie had been her first big mistake. Like they always said, tell one lie and you have to keep covering up. After a week at home, recovering from the bruises and crying on and off, she had returned to school. Tim was so damn careful that he had called a couple of times, asking if she were feeling okay and if she would be back in school soon — the concerned, solicitous boyfriend — and then, once she was back, engineered a noisy "official" break-up. She ended up going out with his friend Randy, a nice — if not overly bright — guy, and Tim would show up with what he and his friends called The Blonde of the Week. She let Randy bring her to the parties; half, she figured, to try and make Tim jealous, and half to punish herself for being so stupid.

Tim was the biggest dealer in the school now, although she and Randy were the only ones who knew that he was the one behind so much of the drug traffic. He was still so damn careful. Then somehow, Peter Mason — a really jerky, ingratiating guy a grade behind them — found out and said that he either wanted a piece of the action or he would tell everything. Randy told her about this, not bright enough to keep *his* mouth shut. Then, one day, Peter freaked out in the cafeteria, what turned out to be a fatal LSD experience. An accident, the police said. Right. But she was too scared of Tim to say anything, and just hoped to God that people would forget the whole thing.

And, except for Colleen Spencer, from her old school, they did. Beverly would never have expected such a vehement reaction from her — Colleen was the beautiful debutante type, the valedictorian of their class, seemingly a perfect human being — one who would surely forget such a sordid incident. But she didn't — asking questions all over the place, obviously determined to find out what really happened. Beverly avoided her whenever she could. Colleen had always made her nervous, asking thoughtful, perceptive questions even when there *wasn't* anything going on. For all her popularity, she tended to be a loner too, hanging out with Patrick Finnegan from their old school, although Beverly was sure that they weren't romantically involved. Maybe Colleen made her nervous because there was something Beverly liked about her. If she hadn't been so perfect, they might have been friends.

But all those questions were making Tim scared — she knew that even *without* Randy telling her. And before Beverly could figure out what to do, the valedictorian of the senior class was found out in front of the school, dead. Another overdose.

Tim had been smart enough to plant drugs in Colleen's locker, and the police decided that Colleen's death, too, had been an accident. Tim also got a few rumors going, and soon, the whole school was convinced that Colleen Spencer had been a secret drug user, possibly even suicidal. Just another tragedy.

Beverly walked through the next week in a daze. A new girl started school, thin and nervous, and Beverly felt sorry for her, remembering what it was like to start school in the middle of the year. For some reason, the girl seemed familiar — maybe it was just the dark eyes, or seeing someone else who looked as if she was always scared, and always pretending not to *be* scared. Tim, always one for the tough, vulnerable type, latched on to her right away, and at first, Beverly didn't do anything, relieved that someone else could be fooled. But she and the girl, Susan McAllister, became friends in an aloof sort of way, and Beverly started trying to warn her, seeing her falling into the same pattern with Tim that she had.

Then, things happened fast. Not only was Patrick Finnegan hanging around Susan, but he was also asking questions. Coming home from school one day and finding Maryanne alone, Beverly almost told her everything, but was afraid to start, afraid to admit all of the lies. But she should have, because Tim was waiting for her after newspaper the next day, dangerously off on angel dust, and she was too afraid *not* to get in the car with him. He drove to a deserted road where they had always gone parking, and proceeded to scare the hell out of her, somehow knowing that she knew everything. He threatened to break her ribs, beat her up, *kill* her if she said anything, making each point with a fist, hitting her in the stomach where it wouldn't show. He threatened and hurt her until she cried, then dumped her out of the car near Harvard Square. For the first time, she knew that he was genuinely insane,

11

and she was much too terrified to tell anyone. Since the injuries didn't show this time, she convinced her father that it was an ulcer attack and spent half the night sick in the bathroom.

She made it to school the next day, too scared to stay home, and it was probably the worst day of her life. Tim was enjoying the power of his threat, and she flinched every time he even looked at her. Unbelievably, during study hall, Susan McAllister started talking about LSD and someone else at the table told her about the two people who had *died* from it — and Patrick Finnegan was asking questions, and everything seemed out of control. Beverly went to her yearbook meeting after school, but she knew she couldn't keep this up anymore. She would have to tell her father everything — let *him* handle it.

Then, Patrick Finnegan "fell" on the stairs, breaking more than one bone. She sat alone in the room where the yearbook staff met, the advisor having sent everyone home; flipping through yearbooks, not sure where to go. There was a yearbook from her old school, and she couldn't help looking through it, seeing pictures of Colleen and Patrick — and there was a picture of Susan standing with Colleen. They were friends. A picture of Colleen and Susan and Patrick. They were all friends. Which meant that Susan and Patrick were asking questions because they *knew* that Tim had killed Colleen, and they were trying to prove it, and — Jesus Christ. She stared at the pictures for a long time, not sure what to do.

Realizing why Patrick had fallen on the stairs and who must have pushed him — *and* knowing that Tim and Randy would be at Tim's house, at the usual afternoon party — Beverly decided to go there. Someone

12

had to stop Tim, and maybe if she showed him the pictures, he would see how crazy it all was and — except, when she got to his house, Susan was there too.

She was so surprised that she just stood there, staring at the three of them, and when Randy came over to see what was wrong with her, she let him see the pictures. Let *him* take the responsibility. Naturally, he panicked, and called Tim out to the hall to see them too. "What do we do? What do we do?" Randy kept saying. "We get rid of her," Tim said, with that strange, scary smile. Beverly was so scared — aware that she was *included* in that threat if she didn't go along — that she almost let them do it. Stood there, watching Tim corner Susan, watching him get ready to kill her. When she finally found enough courage to run out of the room and call the police, she had expected Randy to try and stop her. Instead, just as scared and horrified as she was, he *helped* her call them.

The police got there in time and she told them everything, Randy chiming in, all of them being taken to the station where the interrogations and accusations started. Her father, Tim's parents, *Colleen's* parents, lawyers, police officers, yelling, fear, guilt. She told them everything, over and over, today for the last time. Until the trial, anyway. She had been released that first night into her father's custody and he had barely spoken to her since. He was right to hate her — everyone should hate her. Everyone pretty much did.

Going back to school had been horrible, especially with Susan in all of her classes — a constant reminder of what a coward she had been. She dropped out of her extracurricular activities and even stopped going to lunch, spending that time alone in the library. And even though all the charges against her had been dismissed, because of duress and cooperative testimony and God only knew what else, they would all still hate her. Until the trial, Randy was in a reform school, Tim off being observed in some place for the criminally insane — Jesus. Suicide might be the coward's way out, but maybe she should really do it. Everyone would be a lot better off.

Chapter Three

Maryanne brought her some dinner on a tray, but Beverly's stomach hurt too much to eat it. Even the smell of the food — salad, garlic bread, spaghetti casserole — made her sick and she moved the tray over to her desk, returning to her bed and huddling under the quilt.

Around eight, her father came in, and she sat up, her hands nervous fists. He stood stiffly, arms across his chest, and she didn't look at him, afraid to see his expression.

"You didn't eat your dinner," he said.

"I'm sorry." She swallowed. "I don't feel very well."

"I'm sure you don't." He moved his jaw. "I'm *very* disappointed in you."

She nodded, fear tightening the muscles in her throat. Terrible to be afraid of her own father. She was scared of almost everyone these days.

"The constant lying is the part I really can't — "
He let out his breath. "Well, I don't suppose we need
to go over it again."

She shook her head, still afraid to look up.

"Do you realize how lucky you are? This all could
have been even worse."

She nodded guiltily, unable to repress a shudder at
the thought of being in a reform school or something.

"Well." He sighed. "We're just very lucky."

She nodded, swallowing so she wouldn't cry.

"I know Dr. Benson didn't work out very well," he
said, "but I've arranged for you to see that new man
in Brookline, Samuels. I've heard good things about
him."

She didn't say anything, remembering the silent
hours in Dr. Benson's thickly carpeted office, biting
her cheek so she wouldn't cry, sidestepping his probing
questions.

"Do you have anything to say?" her father asked.

She shook her head.

"Well." He refolded his arms. Communication wasn't
exactly one of the bywords of their relationship.

"Do you" — her voice was smaller and shakier than
she had expected — "want me to leave after my birthday?"

"*Leave*? Where are you going to go?"

"Away," she said. "So you wouldn't have to — I
mean, so I wouldn't be here. I'll be eighteen, so — "

"Don't be stupid," he said sharply. "That's no so-
lution."

"It would be easier for everyone. I mean — "

"Oh, I see," he said, his face tight. "And how would
you live?"

"I don't know." She wiped her eyes with her sleeve. "Does it matter?"

"What do you think?"

She shrugged, hunching against the burning pain starting in her stomach.

"Now, look," he said, low and stern, "it *matters*. It matters a great deal. We're not talking about running away, we're talking about starting over. Pulling yourself together."

She closed her eyes, anticipating the predictable shot of pain across her stomach. Ulcers were scary things. Terrible things. "You don't think it's kind of a lost cause?"

"No," he said, sounding angry. "I don't."

"Yeah, right."

"Now, look," he said. "I know it isn't going to be easy, but — "

"I wish — " She stopped before saying that she wished she had been in the car with her mother. Her father would throw a fit.

"I wish you hadn't been involved either," he said. "But I think we're a little beyond that."

"Yeah," she said.

"Well." He cleared his throat. "I'll be driving you to school in the morning."

She nodded. He always did these days, apparently not even trusting her on public transportation.

"All right then. I'll call you in the morning."

She nodded.

She had more nightmares than usual that night. She had had them pretty regularly since her mother died, but they had gotten much worse after everything happened with Tim. She couldn't always remember the dreams but would wake up either terrified or crying, the blankets tangled around her.

After her father called her, she sat up very slowly, feeling even more tired than she had when she'd finally turned out the light the night before. She rested her face in her hands, not sure if she should try to remember the dream, or just shake it off. A jail. Something about a very dark jail. And Tim, standing on the other side of the bars, smiling that smile, saying, "Trust me. Come on, you can trust me." Then, he was laughing and as she turned away from him, she saw Susan McAllister behind her, smiling the same scary smile, and — shake it off. She should have tried to —

"Beverly?" her father said through the door. "Are you up?"

"Um" — she pulled in a deep breath — "yeah."

"Okay, I just wanted to be sure," he said. "You don't want to be late."

No. She definitely didn't want to walk in late. It was such a small school that everyone knew about the hearing, and they were all going to be waiting, and watching, and — she shook her head. If she thought about it, she wasn't going to be able to make it in there at all.

Since they were expecting a criminal, she was tempted to wear tough clothes — old torn jeans, jeans jacket, her Judas Priest concert T-shirt — but it seemed safer to go the Fair Isle sweater, nice Levi's route and blend in with everyone else. No point in *looking* for attention.

When she got downstairs, her father was at the kitchen table, drinking coffee and reading *The Boston Globe*, with Oliver sitting next to him, crunching through a bowl of Cheerios and chattering happily.

"Good morning," Maryanne said, standing near the stove, pouring herself some coffee.

Beverly nodded. "I'll be in there," she said to her father, indicating the living room.

He sighed, lowering the newspaper. "Shouldn't you eat something?"

"I'm not hungry." She went into the living room, Oliver following her.

"Can we watch cartoons?" he asked, climbing onto the couch next to her.

"Oliver, I — " She let out her breath. She never yelled at Oliver. He was too little to be mean to. "I have to finish some homework, okay? Why don't you go in and eat your breakfast?"

"Will you play with me after school?"

"Yeah, sure, whatever," she said, tying his right sneaker so he wouldn't fall over the lace. "Go eat your cereal, okay?"

"I can tie shoes too," he said.

"I know," she said patiently. "You're very good at it."

"Can I tie yours?"

She lifted her foot onto the couch and he carefully untied the Topsider, slowly retying it with a large neat bow.

"Double knot?" he asked.

"No, thank you."

"Mommy says — "

"Well, she's right," Beverly said. "You'd better go eat your cereal before it's mush."

"Okay."

As he went back to the kitchen, she closed her eyes. This was going to be an awful day.

Her father came out, putting on a tweed jacket and checking through his briefcase. Maryanne walked over to the couch, handing her a lunchbag, as well as a peanut butter sandwich wrapped in a paper towel.

"Eat this on the way," she said. "You'll feel terrible otherwise."

"Thank you," Beverly said, although her stomach hurt too much for her even to think about eating. Her father was kissing Maryanne good-bye and she concentrated on her knapsack, not wanting to see them. It probably shouldn't still bother her to see them being affectionate with each other, but it always did.

"Have a good day," Maryanne said.

That seemed to be directed toward her, so Beverly nodded, going outside after her father.

They drove in silence over the bridge to Cambridge. When her father pulled up in front of the school, she made a production of gathering her things together, her hands shaking.

"It's not going to be as bad as you think it is," he said.

"You sound like *her*."

"I probably do," he agreed. "I want you home right after school."

She nodded, opening the door.

"Beverly?"

"What?"

He shook his head. "Never mind. Have a good day."

"You too," she said mechanically. When she got to the main entrance, she glanced back, seeing him still parked there, looking after her, with his chin resting in his hand. Probably waiting just to make sure she went in. Nothing like trust.

Her legs trembled as she walked down the hall, and

she gripped her knapsack strap tightly. She knew everyone was staring, and conversations stopped when she walked past, resuming in whispers. Her hands were shaking enough to make it hard to open her locker, but she managed, and brought the books she needed down to her homeroom, not looking at anyone.

She could feel hatred and bitterness everywhere — it wasn't just paranoia. Or like that stupid joke — yeah, you're paranoid, and yeah, someone *is* following you. Maryanne humor. She probably heard it at aerobics class.

It wasn't my fault! she wanted to shout. I didn't know he was going to do it, and if I had, I couldn't have stopped him. I'm sorry. I'm really, really sorry.

Instead, she sat stiffly, self-consciously, not sure if people were blaming her personally, or blaming her because Tim — and Randy, for that matter — wasn't around to take the brunt of it. Colleen had been about as popular as it was possible to be.

She focused down at her desk during classes, teeth pressed into her lip, afraid that she was going to cry. Ninth grade all over again. Her stomach hurt, but if she took her medication, someone would probably see her and drag her down to the office for taking drugs. If it got much worse though, she would have to go down to the clinic and take some. The nurse would know that Tagamet wasn't a narcotic.

It was strange to be picked last during gym class. Not that she was the world's greatest athlete or anything, but during a game she always took care of her responsibilities. It was easier than calling attention to herself by screwing up, or refusing to play. Now even Jane Muggins was picked before she was. The team that got stuck with her would exchange glances —

and it really wasn't just paranoia. But the worst thing was that Susan McAllister was in her class. In *all* of her classes. They hadn't spoken since — well, since the night Beverly had almost gotten her killed by telling Tim — Jesus. No wonder the whole school hated her. The blame was pretty clear-cut on *that* one.

Susan tooked terrible — about as bad as Beverly felt — thin, hunched, dark shadows under her eyes, her face very pale against the light pink sweater she was wearing. As if she might be going to cry. Except for Patrick Finnegan, she kept to herself as much as Beverly did, but the difference was that everyone was very kind and supportive around her. Once, during English, their eyes met and Susan seemed to slump, like a little animal who had been kicked once too often; then, her expression stiffened and she looked away. Beverly felt her stomach twist, and stared down at her books, eyes dangerously full of tears.

School ended, finally, and she walked outside. Around her, people were talking and laughing, making after-school plans. Meet in Filene's Basement after the orthodontist, go to a movie in Harvard Square, bake brownies. Bake *brownies*? She had to turn around and look at those two. Tenth-graders. Figured.

Not that she would turn down an opportunity to bake brownies with someone. Even a tenth-grader. Suddenly so lonely that she knew she was going to cry, she veered over to a nearby graffiti-scarred bench. She sat on it, fists tight, eyes closed. Maybe if she had a cigarette. She's probably feel a lot better if she had a —

"Beverly!" A voice said happily.

She looked up, startled. Oliver. "What are you doing

22

here?" She glanced around. "Where's Mary — your mother?"

He pointed to the row of parents' cars in the school driveway.

Beverly frowned. "Why are you guys here?" They only had one car, which meant Maryanne had taken Oliver into Cambridge on the subway, stopped at her father's office at the university — but why would they bother? Unless maybe it was to check up on her.

"To see you!" Oliver said, trying to take her hand. "Come on."

She followed him uneasily, shaking her head when he suggested that she sit up front with them, and climbing into the backseat. Maryanne was wearing a hand-dyed dashiki and jeans. All she needed were some love beads.

"How come you're here?" Beverly asked, suspicious. "I was going to come right home."

Maryanne smiled at her. Didn't anything get the woman down? "We thought you might want to come grocery shopping with us," she said.

"Grocery shopping?" Beverly closed her eyes. Entertainment in her new life, the Life Without Friends. They would probably have to go home and bake brownies. Or snap green beans or something. Jesus.

They went to the Star Market in Porter Square.

"Why didn't you just go to the one in Boston?" Beverly asked.

"I like this one," Maryanne said.

"Well, is it okay if I wait in the car?"

Maryanne glanced at Oliver, who was having a conversation with himself, something about Mr. T. "No, it isn't okay," she said quietly. "I'm not going to *make* you, but it isn't okay."

23

Beverly scowled, but got out of the car. "You're not my mother."

"No," Maryanne agreed. "But I'm much healthier than you are."

"Oh, wow. What are you going to do to me?"

"Force-feeding you would be a start." She held out her hand, checking both ways for cars. "Oliver, come here."

"My name's B.A.!" he barked in a Mr. T. voice. "Bad Attitude!"

Maryanne gave Beverly such an ironic grin that she almost grinned back. "Come here, B.A.," she said, and he took her hand.

Once they were inside, Oliver went up the aisle ahead of them to pick out dog food for Jason, their schnauzer, who was ten years old and a fairly grumpy animal. He was mostly her father's dog.

Beverly slouched after Maryanne and the basket, knowing that she wouldn't be asked to go after anything. "I need some razor blades," she said.

Maryanne barely flinched. "How about some of those disposable shavers?" she asked, scanning her list.

"It's easier with blades," Beverly said.

Maryanne picked out a package of onion rolls.

"Are we having hamburgers or something disgusting tonight?"

"Yes," Maryanne said.

"I hate hamburgers."

"You hate most food."

Beverly shrugged. "Depends on who's doing the cooking."

Maryanne just looked at her.

"Well, it does," Beverly said defensively. "Some people are lousy cooks."

Oliver came back with an armload of Cycle 4, which he dumped into the basket, Maryanne moving the rolls out of the way just in time.

"What now, Mommy?" he asked.

"Well," she said, pointing as they turned down another aisle, "why don't you go get some Special K and some cereal you like?"

He nodded and went off, mumbling gruffly: "Stay in school! Don't cuss yo' mama!"

"He's too young to watch *The A-Team*," Beverly said.

Maryanne put a can of coffee in the basket. "You want to be the one to tell him he can't watch it anymore?"

"It's probably corrupting him."

"Probably," Maryanne agreed, selecting some oatmeal.

Beverly slouched after her. By now, any *normal* person would have slugged her. She had almost never seen Maryanne lose her temper. What a doormat.

"I'm out of cigarettes," she said conversationally.

"Good," Maryanne said. "Maybe you won't get cancer."

"I can smoke if I want. You can't stop me."

"No." Maryanne waited for Oliver to catch up. "But I don't have to encourage you."

"Oh, wow. Power trip." Beverly walked extra-sulkily.

Oliver came back with the cereal and went ahead to get orange juice.

"If you won't give me money," Beverly said, "I'll have to rip them off."

Maryanne shrugged. "I'll have to report you."

"No way. You wouldn't do that."

Maryanne looked at her. "Do you want to take that chance?"

"You hate me, don't you," Beverly said. "I bet you'd report me even if I *didn't* steal anything. I bet you'd plant cigarettes on me just to get me in trouble."

Maryanne laughed.

"I bet you would," Beverly said. Why did she have to be so damned good-natured? Talk about irritating.

Maryanne selected eggs, margarine, milk.

"I bet you'd be *glad* if I got in more trouble, wasn't around anymore."

"But you're such a pleasant shopping companion."

Beverly almost laughed that time.

In the vegetable section, Maryanne got some of almost everything.

"I'm not snapping those," Beverly said as Maryanne put a bag of green beans in the shopping cart.

"Then you can chop the onions."

"I hate onions," Beverly said automatically.

Maryanne grinned. "I know." She took the bag of apples Oliver carried over. "Good job. These are beautiful."

"Can we get pears too?" he asked.

"Sure. Pick out four." She reached up to rip a plastic bag off the roll over the tomatoes and handed it to him.

"I love pears," he said. "Don't you, Beverly?"

Never pick on small people. "Um, yeah," she said. "Pears are good."

"Come help me."

She followed him, avoiding Maryanne's eyes, helping him choose the four best pears. Not too soft, not too hard, nice and shiny.

"Oh, great," Maryanne said when they came back. "What good helpers I have." She looked at Beverly over Oliver's head, her eyes so amused that Beverly grinned wryly. Maryanne would make it a whole lot easier if she weren't likable.

Feeling uncomfortable and claustrophobic in the check-out line, she went outside, sitting on the curb in front of the store, staring out at the parking lot. You knew you were in bad shape when grocery shopping — not even shopping, just tagging along after someone — was a terribly difficult ordeal. A hand came onto her shoulder and she flinched defensively.

"Here." Maryanne gave her a ten-dollar bill. "Why don't you go up and get a new record?"

"What, you mean at Stereo Jack's or something?"

"Sure."

"They only have old records," Beverly said, regretting it the instant she saw Maryanne's unhappy expression.

"Oh. Okay." Her stepmother managed a smile. "It was just an idea." She glanced both ways, took Oliver's hand, and started across the parking lot to the car.

Still holding the ten-dollar bill, Beverly watched them. What would it be like to be young, marry a man you loved very much, have a little boy, and then get stuck with an absolute rat of a stepdaughter? Probably not much fun. She looked at the ten-dollar bill. Why was Maryanne so nice to her? She had no reason to be.

She walked over to the car, where her stepmother was loading bags into the trunk, her back stiff.

"Maryanne," she said quietly.

Her stepmother closed the trunk.

"I, uh — I — " Beverly sighed. She was lousy at this. She folded her arms, hunching over them. "I apologize."

Maryanne also sighed. "You make things harder than they have to be."

Beverly shrugged, kicking at the cement with one shoe.

"Well." Maryanne smiled her little-kid smile, all teeth and happy eyes. "You never used to apologize."

Beverly shrugged.

"Go get a couple of old records, okay? Oliver and I can drive up and meet you."

Beverly kicked the cement. "You don't have to be nice to me."

"You're right," Maryanne said, pushing the shopping cart over next to two others. "I don't."

Chapter
Four

So, life fell into a pattern — a tedious pattern, but a pattern regardless. Get up, go to school, avoid meeting people's eyes or participating in class, come home. Go to her room, listen to music, hang out with Oliver if Maryanne was going to class or something, study, go to bed. Back to Life Before Tim. It wasn't much fun, but there wasn't any pressure either. Sometimes, just for variety, she went for walks. Wow.

Her father drove her to Brookline for her first appointment with Dr. Samuels. God forbid she be allowed to take the T by herself. She might fall into bad company on the way.

When they pulled into the parking lot, next to a square brick building full of dentists, podiatrists, and psychologists, Beverly's stomach jumped nervously, and she clenched her hands under folded arms.

"I'll come in with you," her father said.

"It's not like it's the first time."

"I'll come in anyway."

The office was on the third floor, with a receptionist sitting in the waiting room. A stiff tweedy couple and a mother with a mean-looking little boy were sitting in four of the eight tubular chairs. After making sure that she didn't know them and didn't have to be embarrassed, Beverly focused on her father and the receptionist.

"My daughter has a four-o'clock appointment," he was saying.

"Beverly Johnson?" she asked, and he nodded. "Why don't you take a seat. The doctor will be right with you."

Beverly let her father sit down, then sat perpendicular to him. He didn't *look* embarrassed. He probably was though. What parent wouldn't be? She glanced at the mother gripping her son's wrist as he slouched down, tried to ignore the tweedy couple's tight-lipped, low-voiced quarrel.

"Miss Johnson?" the receptionist said. "You can go down now. Second door on the left."

Beverly stood up, her fists clenched so hard that her fingers were cramping.

"You don't have to stay," she said to her father.

"I'd rather," he said, and picked up a *National Geographic*.

Dr. Samuels' door was open and she stopped uneasily, seeing a man with dark curly hair and glasses sitting behind a crowded, yet orderly desk.

"Hi," he said, standing up. "You must be Beverly. Come in." Cream-colored shirt, maroon crewneck, grey flannel pants. Loafers, probably.

"Come in," he said again. "Sit down."

She nodded, prepared not to like him.

He came over and ushered her in, closing the door behind them. Brown loafers, well worn. Late thirties, three children, fluttery bespectacled wife. Brandeis, undergrad; Columbia graduate. Maybe Brown.

She looked around the room. Bookshelves, dark paneling, green shag carpet. There was a couch and two easy chairs, a coffee table with a bowl of daisies. A *man* with daisies? She frowned. Also, a box of Kleenex. She sure as hell wouldn't be using any. A small refrigerator in the corner, a coffee machine above it. What looked like a box of muffins next to it. She glanced at him, seeing a bit of a stomach bulge. Definitely a box of muffins.

"Sit anywhere you like," he said.

Did that include the waiting room? She selected the tubular chair across from his desk.

"You want some coffee?" he asked. "Tea? Soda?"

She shook her head.

He sat down behind his desk, taking a sip from a brown pottery mug. Father's day. Or Sunday afternoon at Quincy Market. "Cigarette?" he asked, lighting one himself.

"What kind?"

"Newport."

She shook her head. "No. Thank you."

He opened his desk drawer. "Marlboros? Salem Lights? Camels?"

She leaned forward. There were, indeed, several brands in the drawer. She sat back. "What do you do, pick up samples on the street?"

He smiled. "What do you think?"

"I think you get patients upset and steal their cigarettes when they're distracted."

31

He laughed. "Maybe so." He held out a pack of Vantages. "Would you like one of Mrs. Murphy's cigarettes?"

"Is that supposed to be funny?"

"Is it?"

"Not really." She frowned. "Aren't you not supposed to mention patients' names?"

"Sorry. Just a joke."

"Oh." She shifted her position, the chair uncomfortable.

"I hear you've been accepted at some very good schools," he said.

She shrugged. Apparently, admission committees didn't read *The Globe* much because she had been accepted almost everywhere she applied: Wesleyan, Smith, Bowdoin, Sarah Lawrence, Middlebury. She didn't get into Yale; she hadn't applied to Harvard.

"Do you know where you want to go?"

She shrugged. Her father was probably going to pull strings, get her into B.U. or Northeastern, and make her live at home. He would *never* trust her to go away to school, not anymore. He hadn't said so, but she could tell.

"What are you interested in studying?" Dr. Samuels asked.

"I'm not, particularly."

He nodded. "It's easier that way. Take different courses, see what you like."

Beverly shrugged.

"It probably wasn't your idea to come here, was it?"

"No," she said.

"How do you feel about it?"

She looked at him, her expression carefully blank.

"Relax," he said. "Okay?"

32

She clenched her hands less visibly. "I look nervous?"

"A little." He lit another cigarette and she repressed an urge to ask him for one. "Does this bother you?"

She shook her head.

"Do you want to tell me something about yourself?"

"No."

'We could talk about the Red Sox."

"I don't like baseball," she said. Actually, she didn't care one way or the other. Her father was a rabid fan, and went to every game he could. Even when he had been teaching at Dartmouth, before the divorce, he had driven down to Fenway Park all the time. She and her mother would go too sometimes, when Beverly was old enough, and she had kind of enjoyed —

"What *do* you like?" Dr. Samuels asked.

She shrugged. How long was this going to be, fifty minutes? He would probably go for fifty-five. Give them their money's worth, goddamn it.

"There isn't anything you want to talk about?"

She shook her head.

Silence.

"Why do you think your father wanted you to come here?" he asked.

She glanced at him. Was he playing stupid, or was this some kind of test to see her reaction, or what? "Well, now, I guess you'd have to ask him, wouldn't you," she said, her voice bored.

He tapped the ashes off the end of his cigarette. "Beverly, once you come in here, he isn't involved anymore. All of this is completely confidential."

"Oh," she said. Yeah, sure. Like her father wouldn't be on the phone bright and early tomorrow morning.

"I'm telling you the truth."

33

She shrugged. "What time is it?"

"Twenty past."

She couldn't hold back a sigh.

"You're not enjoying this?"

"Give me a break," she said. "I really don't want to be here."

"Where would you be otherwise?"

She shrugged.

"Where would you *like* to be?"

Not that she was going to answer him, but she couldn't think of anyplace, except maybe places that would have changed the course of events, like in the car with her mother, or — she shuddered. Maybe she really *did* need help.

"Where?" he asked gently.

Her eyes felt hot, as if she were going to cry, so she kept her head down, biting her cheek and remembering the hours of sitting in Dr. Benson's office, barely speaking.

"Beverly?"

She tensed the muscles in her right leg, then her left. "You'll tell my father."

"Never."

He *sounded* sincere. "You'll think I'm crazy, or — I don't know. Something bad will happen."

He shook his head, and she studied his expression. She might as well tell him. If something bad was going to happen, why put it off? "I wish I wasn't anywhere," she said. "I wish I had been in the car with my mother." She didn't explain further — her father would have told him about the "accident." She folded her arms, waiting for his reaction. "You probably think that's really bad."

He shook his head.

"It would have been a lot easier."

"For you?"

She shrugged. "For everyone."

"You don't think it would have upset people?"

Oh, yeah. Thousands. "Who?" she asked. "Except for my father, maybe. And he'd be over it by now. *Long* since."

He looked at her thoughtfully. "Do you really think so?"

"Yeah, I think so," she said, irritated. "What, you want me to say things just so you can disagree?"

"No. Of course not." He inhaled, exhaled smoke. "Would your not being here have changed things?"

Things. "What, you mean with Tim?"

He nodded. Her father had definitely given him the blow-by-blow.

"I don't know." She thought about that. The *same* thing might not have happened, but Tim was such a psychopath that someday, sometime, he would have — "I don't know. Probably not."

"What about now?" he asked. "Where do you go from here?"

She sighed. This was really a drag. "I don't know. Home for dinner probably."

His eyes flickered. Amusement, she thought. "And after that?"

"I'll probably study, and then I'll go to bed."

"What about tomorrow?"

She gritted her teeth. "What do you want me to do, plot the rest of my life, hour by hour?"

"Do you think about it?"

This guy was really starting to get on her nerves.

"No, I'm a *carpe diem* kind of person," she said, and was even more irritated when he grinned. "I wasn't being funny."

"You're just extremely intelligent."

"Oh, yeah. Right." She tilted her head to try and see his watch. Was she ever going to get out of here?

"How do you and your stepmother get along?" he asked.

"Oh, for God's sakes." She closed her eyes, very tired of this conversation.

"You don't want to talk about it?"

"No. I don't want to talk about it."

"How about your father?"

Her father probably didn't want to talk about it either. She rubbed her hand across her stomach, warning pains cutting through the extra dose of medicine she had taken before coming. "Look, it really isn't any of your business."

He shrugged. "Okay. We'll talk about something else."

"Great." A headache was starting too. "Is it time for me to leave yet?"

"Not quite." He took a sip from his mug. "Do you want to come back here on Thursday?"

"No."

"Well, how about a week from today?"

"Do I have a choice?"

"I don't know," he said. "You'll have to talk to your father about that."

Translation: No. "Great. I'll hold my breath."

"Is it me personally?" he asked. "Or psychology in general?"

"I don't know. A little of both, I guess."

His eyes were very receptive.

"I don't know." She shifted in the chair. "It's a waste of money. I mean, it's not like I'm going to talk to you or anything."

He shrugged. "You might change your mind."

Yeah, right. Don't hold your breath.

"There's no pressure," he said.

Maybe he was divorced. Who could stand to live with him?

"Well." He looked at his watch. "I guess it's about time."

She stood — almost jumped — up, heading for the door. He came right with her, surprisingly quick. He held out his hand and she shook it, not sure what else to do.

"I'll see you next week," he said.

She withdrew her hand. "Maybe."

"How was it?" her father asked, once they were in the car.

"Do I have to go back?"

"You have to go to *someone*. Not necessarily him."

She slouched down, staring straight ahead.

"Did you not like him?"

She shrugged. "It's a waste of money."

Her father also shrugged. "Then, I'll waste my money."

"Whatever." She closed her eyes so he wouldn't yell at her for having a sulky expression.

"If you want to look around for someone else, we can."

"I don't care."

Her father's face tightened. "This is a little too important for you not to care."

"Yeah, well, I don't."

He started the car, reversing abruptly and driving out of the parking lot. She knew he was angry, but didn't feel like worrying about it. He was always angry at her. They didn't speak again until he parked the car in the spot behind their brownstone.

"Wait a minute," he said, and she took her hand off the doorhandle. He didn't speak right away and she looked at him, noticing that the knuckles of his right hand were white. They were alike that way — very tense people. Stubborn, withdrawn, distant people. Sometimes she wondered what Maryanne had seen in the tall, taciturn professor; quiet and achievement-oriented. But, he was different around her: happier, more relaxed, less stiff. It was when she saw the two of them and Oliver together, all smiling and comfortable, that she felt the most left out. Like the standardized tests with the "which one of these objects doesn't belong" questions.

"Beverly, I'm not doing this to make you more unhappy," he said. "I really think it will help you."

She nodded. "And take the responsibility off you."

"You know that's not fair."

She shrugged, studying her hands. Not very attractive hands; small and clenched. She only acted like her father; she *looked* like her mother. Dark deep-set eyes, shoulder-length brown, almost black hair, average height, somewhat underweight. Unhealthy-looking.

"Well." Her father took the keys out of the ignition. "Apparently, you don't want to discuss it."

She got out of the car, pausing to tie her shoe so she could lag behind him.

"Are you coming?" he asked.

Did she have a choice?

Chapter Five

The next Tuesday, she went back to Samuels, Mary-anne driving this time, Oliver home with Mrs. Mont-gomery.

"Do you want me to come up with you?" her step-mother asked.

"No." Beverly opened the door. "You don't even have to wait."

"Waste a free hour? Are you kidding?" She held up a copy of Anne Tyler's newest book. "I *want* to wait."

Beverly shrugged. Good old everything-for-the-best Maryanne. When she went in, Dr. Samuels was eating a blueberry muffin.

"Want one?" He indicated the box.

"No, thank you."

"I shouldn't myself," he said. "My wife says it's a bad habit to get into."

Beverly decided that it would be rude to agree. *Too* rude. There were limits.

"Would you like a soda? Anything?"

She shook her head.

"Well, if you change your mind." He sat down in one of the easy chairs.

"I'd rather sit over here."

"Sure," he said. "But I'm going to sit over here, okay?"

Trying to make a fool out of her. She sat in the other easy chair, legs crossed, arms folded.

"So." He smiled at her. "How's everything going?"

"Great," she said. "My whole life's turned around. I guess I won't have to come here anymore."

"Well, that sounds terrific. Tell me about it."

"Yeah, right." She brought her leg up onto the chair, wrapping her arms around it.

"So, things aren't great?"

"What do you think?"

"Well, tell me about it."

"Maybe I don't want to."

"What *do* you want to do?"

She hugged her knee closer. "You're a very repetitive person, you know that? You must drive your wife crazy."

"Sometimes," he agreed cheerfully.

"Do you use this approach all day long? You must get sick of it."

"Sometimes."

"Yeah, you must. I already am." She rubbed her sweater sleeve across her face.

"You look tired," he said.

"Boy, you're really sharp. Did you go to Harvard or something?"

"Columbia."

40

She laughed.

"What's so funny?"

"Nothing. Brandeis undergrad?"

"Tufts."

One out of two, not bad.

"Making a cliché out of me?" he asked.

"Yeah, I guess." Her left leg was getting cramped and she brought her right one up on the chair instead.

"How's school?"

"Great."

"That's good to hear."

"Like I said, everything's great."

He nodded.

"So I can stop coming here."

"Is it that bad?"

"It's a pain." She held back a yawn, very tired.

"Late night?"

"Not really." She had had the usual nightmares, bad as ever. Or worse than ever, depending on how you looked at it. Tim was there, walking after her with the relaxed, malicious smile. Colleen Spencer was there too, the good-humored blonde model looks strangely flattened, almost zombie-like. Tim was after both of them, except Colleen was going to help him, and — she had woken up crying, the sheets and blankets twisted.

"Your face is more expressive than you think it is."

She shrugged.

"People must be treating you differently."

"Which people?"

"Teachers, your friends."

She hugged her leg more tightly. "Maybe I don't have any."

"Friends?"

41

"No," she said. "Teachers. What do you think?" She shook her head. "Jesus."

"Does it bother you?"

"I like it."

"Why?"

"Because I do."

"Who do you talk to?"

She moved her jaw. "Maybe I don't."

"Do you like it that way?"

She nodded.

"Well." He picked up his mug. "That's what's important. Your being happy."

"Yeah."

"Are you happy?"

"Deliriously," she said.

"That's what's important."

"Yeah."

He took a pack of cigarettes out of his shirt pocket, lighting one. "I quit smoking over the weekend," he said conversationally. "Not doing too well, am I?"

"Doesn't look that way."

"I guess I'm just not motivated enough." He rested the cigarette in an ashtray on the coffee table. "Starting is a lot easier than stopping."

Was he being profound or offhand? It was hard to tell.

"What do you do in your free time?" he asked.

"Crusade against smoking."

He laughed. "Seriously."

"What, you mean, do I have any 'hobbies'?"

"Sure."

Hobbies. What a jerk. "I make Christmas ornaments out of shells."

"Really?" He looked interested. "What kind of ornaments?"

Total jerk. "Your basic. I make macrame plant holders too." She checked his expression. Still interested. What a dolt. "Then, I sell them at local craft shows."

"Sounds like fun," he said.

"Oh, yeah. Lots." Was he really that stupid? He couldn't be. She didn't *think*. "I also collect leaves."

"Very industrious," he said.

"I like to keep busy."

"Good for you."

It was quiet, and then he laughed. Well, good. She had been worried there for a minute.

"What's so funny?" she asked. "My hobbies are very important to me."

He nodded.

"You shouldn't make fun of people. If those were really my hobbies, I'd probably be set back years."

"Probably."

"That's a hell of a chance to take." She sighed. "What time is it?"

"Twenty-five past."

"Is that *all*?" She covered her eyes with her arm, wishing that she could sleep.

"How did it happen?"

"How did what happen?" She lowered her arm. "You mean, the stuff with Tim?"

He nodded.

"Don't you read the paper?"

"The newspaper doesn't always tell the whole story," he said.

She shrugged, feeling her face tighten.

"You don't want to tell me about it?" he said and asked.

"Boy, you're really perceptive," she said. "Is that why you decided to go into psychology?"

43

"I like to talk to people," he said.

"Upset them, more likely." She pointed to the coffee table. "That's not the same box of Kleenex you had last week. Did you make that many people cry?"

"No. I have allergies."

"Yeah, sure." She twisted in the chair, just wanting to get *out* of this place.

"Have you decided where you're going to school?"

What a mosquito. "University of Arkansas."

"Good school," he said.

She had to stare at him. "Do you think you're funny or something?"

"Do you?"

"No."

"When do you have to let schools know?" he asked.

"Pretty soon."

"You got in — where?"

"Smith, Bowdoin, Wesleyan, Middlebury, Sarah Lawrence." Maybe it was twenty of five now. Maybe.

"Do you have a first choice?"

"I don't think I'm going to go to any of them."

"Take some time off?"

She realized that she was knotting her hands together and abruptly relaxed them. "I think I'll be going to school around here. Live at home and stuff."

"Why?"

"Why." She let out a hard breath. "You're really boring, you know that? Have you been married long?"

"Six years," he said, his expression amused.

"Hard to believe."

"I gather you don't want to go away to school?"

"No, I — I mean, they won't let me."

"They?"

"My father. Who do you think?" She shook her

head. He brought new dimensions to the word "daft."

"Have you talked to him about it?"

"I don't *have* to talk to him. I know what he thinks."
She leaned forward to try and see his watch. "Can I
go yet?"

"No."

"It must be almost time."

"Almost," he agreed. "Why doesn't he want you to
go away to school?"

"How should I know?" she asked defensively. "Because he doesn't trust me. He wants to keep an eye
on me."

Dr. Samuels nodded.

"If I go away, I'll just get in more trouble."

"He thinks," Dr. Samuels said.

"Yeah. I mean — " She stopped. How was he trick-
ing her into talking? She didn't want to talk. "I don't
know," she said, more quietly.

"But you want to go away."

"Well — yeah. Of course." Except she didn't. Lousy
as it was at home, it was easier than leaving. The more
she thought about it, the scarier —

"Beverly?"

She looked up.

"*Do* you want to go away to school?"

"What do you think?" she asked. "Look, can I go
now?"

He checked his watch. "You should talk to your
father about this."

"Don't tell me what to do!"

"It's only a suggestion."

"Yeah, right." She scowled. "Can I go now?"

He nodded. "Have a good week."

"Oh, yeah," she said. "Absolutely."

Chapter
Six

Dinner was quiet. She played with her food, eating just enough to keep from getting yelled at. Oliver was chattering about kindergarten and how they had been reading, and boy, he knew *every* word. Maryanne and her father were saying pleased parent things, and Oliver got so wound-up that he knocked over his milk. He started to cry, Maryanne blotting the tablecloth with her napkin and pouring him a fresh third of a glass while her father got some paper towels and cleaned up the rest of the mess.

"May I be excused?" Beverly asked when things had calmed down.

Her father glanced at her plate. "Are you finished?"

"Yes."

"Well, don't waste that meat — give it to Jason."

She nodded, seeing her father and Maryanne exchange glances as she stood up. No, she wasn't anorexic — she just wasn't hungry. Was that such a crime?

She cut the chicken into small pieces — Jason was old enough to be having trouble with his teeth — and dumped it into his dish, Jason waddling over to eat it, tail wagging.

"Dumb dog." She patted him. Dogs who didn't come up to your knees were stupid-looking.

She went up to her room, passing swiftly through the dining room, and closed the door behind her. She paused by the stereo, in a bad enough mood to put on the Dead Kennedys. Loud.

She sat down on the bed. Another exciting evening. School nights were at least better than weekends — she could kill a lot of time with homework. On weekends, you were *supposed* to be out.

What was Tim doing right now? With her luck, escaping. She wasn't sure what places for the criminally insane were like: cells with bars, or just hospital rooms with locks? If she woke up in the middle of the night, she worried about him coming after her, but he probably wasn't that stupid. If they ran into each other on the street someday, he would probably hurt her, but if he got out now, he would head for California or Texas or someplace. Somewhere safe.

His being smart made him scarier. Like she knew he never made a threat unless he was sure he could carry it out. She had half expected him to shout something in the courtroom, or send her a scary letter or something, but knowing him, he was going out of his way to show the authorities that he was "psychologically on the mend." His lawyers hadn't been able to keep him from being incarcerated until the trial, but Beverly knew that they were probably preparing some kind of "temporary derangement due to substance abuse"

47

defense. She was pretty sure that they would never be able to pull it off since there were enough witnesses to prove that he had premeditated —

"Beverly," her father said through the door. "May I come in?"

She turned the stereo down and sat in her desk chair. "Yeah."

He opened the door. "Am I interrupting you?"

She shook her head.

"How did it go today?"

She shrugged.

"Do you like him any better?"

"He's okay," she said, without enthusiasm. He was a lot better than the first guy she had gone to.

"Do you think you should go twice a week?"

"Maybe I should just check into an asylum," she said.

"You know I don't mean it that way."

"Oh."

"Come on, Beverly. Let's not fight." He leaned against the door, hands in his pockets, but still stiff. "It's almost May. You have to make a decision about school so we can get the deposit check in."

She stared at him, startled out of her slouch. "You mean, he called you?"

"Who?"

"Did you call Samuels to check up on me?"

Her father looked confused. "Beverly, what are you talking about?"

Maybe she had sort of jumped the gun. "I guess I made a mistake."

"Did you and Dr. Samuels talk about college today?"

"Not really."

"Well, we have to decide pretty quickly. You don't

48

want to be sitting here next September with no place to go."

She touched the top of her desk, the surface very clean and shiny. She wasn't one for clutter.

"Beverly?"

"No, sir," she said. "I don't."

"I didn't think so." He took off his glasses, rubbing the bridge of his nose. "Before — well, I guess you'd decided that Wesleyan was your first choice."

She shrugged.

"And what was your second, Smith?"

"Yale."

"Okay," he said, "but Smith would come next."

"Yes, sir."

He frowned and put the glasses back on. "Do you still feel the same way?"

"I don't know."

"Well, why don't you look over the catalogs, think about it, and we can talk tomorrow night."

She shrugged affirmatively.

"Do you want to visit any of them again?"

She shook her head.

"Well. All right, then." His hands went back into his pockets. "Are you going to watch *The A-Team* with us?"

Beverly let herself grin. That would be great to have on film: The professor, in his tweeds, off to watch Mr. T.

"Well." He opened the door. "That's where we'll be."

"Dad?"

He turned, looking at her over the glasses.

"What if, uh, something happens and I end up not going? Do you lose the deposit?"

49

"Why wouldn't you go?"

"I don't know." She didn't look at him. "I mean, just in case."

"Just in case what?"

"I don't know. Just in case."

"Well." He frowned. "It isn't *that* much money. Although I certainly don't anticipate your not going."

She sighed.

"It's always been my understanding that you *wanted* to go away to school."

"Yeah, I guess."

"Well, then." He cleared his throat in obvious discomfort. "I don't think staying here and going to school would be advisable."

"You want to get rid of me, right?"

"I just don't think it would be a healthy situation."

In other words: You'll be eighteen, we don't want you anymore.

"Beverly, I think going away to school will be the best thing that ever happened to you."

It couldn't be much *worse*, anyway.

"I'm afraid I really don't understand," he said. "Do you want to talk about it?"

She shook her head.

"Beverly — "

She took her French book out of her knapsack, opening it to her homework assignment. "Oliver will be upset if you miss the beginning of the show."

Her father glanced at his watch. "I really don't think he — are you sure you don't want to discuss it?"

She nodded, pulling a piece of looseleaf paper from her left drawer.

"Well. Read the catalogs, okay?"

She nodded, starting to translate a piece by Sartre.

She went from that, to her physics, to her English essay, only coming out for a glass of caffeine-free Coke. She wasn't supposed to drink caffeine.

Back in her room, she finished the English essay, then wrote out the extra-credit history "Thought Questions" at the end of the Cold War chapter. Even when things had been at their worst, she had always been careful to do her work well. Writing neatly, carefully, using clean looseleaf paper, carrying the finished homework in folders so it wouldn't get wrinkled. Tim had always made fun of her for it.

When she was finished, it was time for the news. She kind of liked to watch the news, hear about what was going on. Most of the television she watched was news.

Maryanne was the only one in the living room, folded up in the corner of the couch, reading. She was very close to her PhD in history, but took courses in all kinds of things: philosophy, religion, literature. Even science. Right now, she was plowing through a thick book called *A Theory of Justice*.

She lowered her book, smiling. "How's the work coming?"

"Fine." Beverly shifted her weight. "Do you mind if I watch the news?"

"Of course not."

Beverly turned on the television, keeping the volume low. Oliver would be asleep and her father was probably in the study, working. She moved to sit in the rocking chair — she always sat in the rocking chair — but hesitated, kind of wanting to sit on the couch. Lately, the rocking chair seemed very isolated.

"Why don't you sit over here?" Maryanne suggested. "That old thing is so uncomfortable."

Beverly sat on the couch, in the other corner. But it wasn't quite eleven and she felt awkward. "Um, I'm going to get more Coke."

Maryanne nodded.

"I meant, um, do you want anything while I'm in there?"

"Oh. Thank you. I'll have some too."

Beverly nodded, going out to the kitchen, filling two glasses. She returned as the news was starting and they sat, drinking Coke, not speaking until the first commercial.

"It's always so depressing," Maryanne said.

Beverly nodded.

"I hope the Red Sox have a good year. It would make your father so happy."

Beverly nodded. It was probably her turn to say something. "Is that a good book?"

"It's an interesting perspective. I'm not sure if I agree with him."

"What about the one you were reading before?"

"Oh, I enjoyed it very much — she's wonderful. It's on the hall table if you want it."

Beverly nodded. Maryanne was big on encouraging reading, and when she finished a book she thought Beverly would enjoy or should read, she would leave it on the hall table. Although she didn't admit it, Beverly generally always read them and Maryanne kept the table well supplied. A typical household ritual.

"I suppose you'll major in English," her stepmother said.

What was this, Bug Beverly about College Day? "Maybe."

The news ended and Maryanne closed her book,

getting ready to leave, but then looked at Beverly and settled herself more comfortably.

"You can go to bed if you want," Beverly said.

"Would you rather be alone?"

No. God, no. Beverly shook her head.

"We could look at *Nightline*."

Beverly nodded.

"Be right back." Maryanne went into the kitchen and Beverly heard her rummaging around, the unmistakable clink of the cookie jar lid. She came back with a plate of oatmeal chocolate chip cookies some friend of hers had made. "Want some?"

Beverly took one. "Thank you."

"Thank Davina."

What a name. Maryanne always seemed to know people with weird names — Beverly wouldn't be surprised to walk in and meet a Bathsheba someday. It was funny that she had so many freaky friends; they all thought Maryanne was incredibly straight — married to a tenured Harvard professor, for God's sakes.

"Were people you know horrified when you married my father?" she asked.

"Well, it's a different sort of lifestyle," Maryanne said. "I guess I was always — I don't know — on the flighty side."

" 'Flighty'?"

"Impractical. Impetuous. Irresponsible." Maryanne grinned, looking much younger. "All those I's."

Beverly thought about that. Maryanne really wasn't any of those things, in spite of her flower-child appearance. When she thought about it, she didn't know all that much about Maryanne — she had never wanted to know. Like, pretend it isn't there, and maybe it will go away.

53

"I guess I've changed a lot in the last six years," Maryanne said. "At least, I hope so."

Six years. Hard to believe. "Has it really been that long?" Beverly asked.

Maryanne nodded carefully. Tactfully.

That made Beverly think about her mother, which Maryanne would have been avoiding, and her eyes filled with tears. She tried never to think about her because even though it had been three years since the accident, she always cried. She had thought that she would at least get over the crying. She lowered her eyes, not wanting Maryanne to see.

"Maybe it just *seems* longer," her stepmother said, and Beverly could tell that she was making the joke to distract her.

"Yeah," she said, whisking the napkin across her eyes.

Maryanne reached over to touch her shoulder, and Beverly sat very still, almost wanting a hug. She had never hugged Maryanne, and she hadn't hugged her father since the couple of months after her mother died. Oliver was a hugger, but he was so bouncy and happy about it that he didn't make her nervous. This, however, did. She leaned away from her stepmother's hand and Maryanne withdrew.

"It's pretty late," Beverly said uneasily. "I think I'd better go to bed."

"What about — ?" Maryanne indicated the television with her eyes.

"N-no. I think I'd better" — she could still feel tears — "go to bed."

Maryanne also stood up, handing her some cookies. "At least take these with you."

"No, I — I mean — " She looked at her stepmother, but broke the gaze, unnerved by how much she wanted this person — this person she had never let herself like — to hug her. To not hate her. She started crying, unexpectedly hard, and had to run upstairs, slamming her bedroom door behind her before remembering that Oliver was asleep. She leaned against the door, waiting for someone to come yell at her. But no one did, and she turned off the light, took off her jeans and climbed into bed, crying under the pillow so no one would hear her.

Chapter
Seven

She was too embarrassed to go down for breakfast the next morning and stayed in her room, waiting for her father to be ready to go. He appeared in the doorway, wearing a surprisingly bright red V-neck sweater under his grey jacket. Maryanne thought he needed to perk up his wardrobe and was always giving him things like suspenders and colorful tartan scarves. Snazzy, her father would say, in a voice somewhere between embarrassment and pleasure.

"Running late?" he asked.

"Yeah," she said, her physics book open as if she were doing last-minute work.

"Well, I really don't like your going off without any breakfast. Come have something to eat and I'll write you a note."

The thought of walking into class with everyone looking at her, instead of getting there first and sitting quietly in the back, was terrifying. "I can't. I have a test first period."

"Well, get something to eat in the car then."

Facing Maryanne was far preferable to facing a staring, hostile class. "Okay."

Maryanne was putting the breakfast dishes in the dishwasher while Oliver sat at the table, singing to himself and playing with the raisins in his cereal. Must be nice to be that young.

"Good morning," Maryanne said.

"Uh, yeah." Beverly blushed, not wanting to, and looked away.

"Do you want a sandwich to take in the car?"

Sandwiches were lunch food. The idea of anything but breakfast food for breakfast right now was nauseating. "Do we have any granola bars?"

"No, but I can pick some up today."

"It's not a big deal." She took two half-pieces of wheat toast from the plate on the table.

"Mommy said we could buy Pop-Tarts," Oliver said, giggling slightly.

Maryanne turned. "When did I say that?"

He didn't answer, practically falling out of his chair with giggles. Must be *very* nice to be that young.

"Bye," Beverly said, wrapping her toast in a napkin.

"Are you going to buy lunch today?" Maryanne asked.

She nodded, although she would go to the library, as always.

"Do you need money?"

She shook her head. "Bye."

She made it to school just in time, slipping into homeroom unnoticed. She sat down, immediately opening the Anne Tyler book from the hall table, listening to everyone talk about college. Cambridge,

57

Massachusetts: the land of one-track minds. Just about all of them had decided — Dartmouth, Syracuse, Georgetown, Conn College, Smith. She glanced up to see who was going to Smith. Debbie Harris, who had been one of Colleen's closer friends. Okay, that cut Smith out. She couldn't go somewhere where the past was going to be dredged up all the time. Probably bunches of Baldwin people would be going to Wesleyan. Sarah Lawrence would be her safest choice. Also, her last choice. Too weird.

What she *really* had to find out was where Susan and Patrick were going. Like, she should go to college in another *country*, if possible. Only, who could she ask to find out?

School was lousy. School was always lousy. She had gym last period — they played badminton, oh yeah, lots of fun. She got stuck with Jane Muggins. Or vice versa.

When class was over, she took her time dressing, then sat in the locker room for a while so the halls would be cleared out when she left.

Finally, she stood up. If she were late getting home, there would be trouble. Not that her father would be there, but Maryanne would probably tell him. As she started to open the locker room door, Susan McAllister came hurrying in. They stopped, both stiffening.

"I-I'm sorry," Beverly said. "I was just — I mean — "

"I left my — " Susan also broke off her sentence and they stared at each other in tense confusion, Susan looking as scared as Beverly felt. Then, Susan moved past her and into the locker room, shoulders hunched protectively.

Beverly was going to leave, *run* even, but that seemed — it wasn't — hesitantly, she went back inside, to the row where Susan's locker was.

"Susan?" she asked, very tentative.

Susan jumped, several expressions seeming to flash across her face before she settled on nervous irritation. "What do you want?" she asked.

Beverly swallowed, unreasonably — maybe — scared. "I'm sorry. I have to ask you something."

Susan didn't say anything, waiting, eyes on her locker.

"Where are you going to school next year?"

Susan looked up. *"What?"*

"Um, I was wondering where you were going to school."

"Williams."

Thank God. "What about Patrick?"

"Yale."

Beverly nodded, relieved. She was safe.

"I suppose you got into Brown," Susan said bitterly. "They have an empty place."

Colleen Spencer had been accepted at Brown, early decision.

"I didn't even apply there," Beverly said, keeping her voice steady.

Susan blinked a few times, looking away, her hands fluttering into her locker to get her book.

"I'm sorry, I — " Beverly let out her breath. Incredible that this was the only person in the school who would really understand why she had to ask this. "D-do you know if anyone's going to Wesleyan?"

Susan glanced at her, also recognizing the irony or *something* of the situation. "Jay Goldberg," she said. "And I think, Shirley Lassiter."

A hockey jock and a chorale star. No one to worry about. "Thank you," Beverly said. "I'm sorry, I — I'm sorry."

It was awkwardly silent.

"I — " Beverly swallowed. "I really couldn't have done anything, you know."

Susan sighed, sitting down on the bench in front of her locker. "All you had to do was *tell* someone," she said quietly.

"I thought — I mean, he — " Beverly stopped. "Yeah, I could have done that," she said, even more quietly. There didn't seem to be anything else to say and she walked, almost ran, out of the locker room, letting the door swing loudly shut behind her.

She told her father that maybe Wesleyan would be okay. He nodded, in evident relief, and probably mailed the check five minutes later. They *were* cutting it close.

Having spoken to Susan took at least some of the pressure off, and while she would still go the other way if she saw her coming, the fear of walking around a corner and running into her by accident wasn't as bad.

Besides, school — terrible as it was — was better than weekends. At least school was something to do, somewhere she had to be. The freedom, and subsequent emptiness, of weekends was scary, Saturday and Sunday were so damned *long*. Maryanne was always thinking of projects — I know, let's refinish the rocking chair! — but Beverly rarely felt comfortable enough to participate.

It was Saturday, and she paced around most of the morning, even sitting to watch cartoons with Oliver.

Horrible cartoons. Whatever happened to *Felix the Cat?* She could maybe go to a movie, but she would feel like a social deviant going by herself. She probably *was* a social deviant, but there was no point in going out of her way to feel like one.

The Red Sox were out of town, so her father was installed in front of the television, Oliver sitting next to him on the couch, scribbling crayoned pictures on thick manila paper.

"Zoe and I are going up to work on the garden," Maryanne said, tying her hair back with a light blue bandanna. "Do you want to come?"

Beverly grinned, managing not to ask if Chloe would be there. Did Maryanne know any Chloes? At any rate, she and Zoe and this other friend of theirs, Irving, had applied for a garden plot in the Fenway — the city had to approve you and everything. The combined plots were called the Victory Gardens — Beverly thought that they had been started during World War II, some sort of morale thing, but she wasn't sure. Zoe had wanted to plant vegetables, but they ended up putting in flowers mostly.

"Are you sure you don't want to come?" Maryanne asked.

Beverly shook her head. She wasn't really into nature. Especially not elbow deep. She went up to her room and looked at her records, not in the mood to hear any of them. And Christ, she couldn't take another afternoon at the library. She went back to the living room.

"Dad?" she asked. "Is it okay if I go for a walk?"

He glanced up, wearing old loafers, flannel slacks, and an untucked button-down shirt. Casual, yet professorial. "Where?"

"I don't know," she said. "Around. I won't be gone long."

He nodded, attention returning to the game.

Feeling lonely, she almost asked Oliver if he wanted to come, but he seemed so happily occupied that she didn't. Jason, sound asleep and wheezing, probably wouldn't be interested, either.

She put on sneakers, decided it was too warm for a sweater, changed her mind at the front door, and went back for one. She felt safer inside a lot of clothes. Maryanne had left a book by Alison Lurie on the hall table, and Beverly took that with her, in case she got bored. Most of the time, when she went on walks, she would go to the library, or end up sitting on a bench in the Public Gardens. The Public Gardens were very pretty.

Outside, she walked down Marlborough Street, taking a right on Exeter Street. The Back Bay was one of Boston's nicest sections — lots of red brick brownstones and a surprising number of trees. Not that Beverly was really keen on cities, but Boston was probably all right. She walked over to Boylston Street, toward the John Hancock Building, one of Boston's two tall buildings. Compared to New York or someplace, it was a pretty stupid-looking skyline.

She was going to go into a store but didn't bother. It was depressing to wander around in stores alone, espcially when salespeople thought you were a shoplifter. They always thought she was a shoplifter, not that she had ever particularly taken anything. Jewelry, a couple of times. Not even very pretty jewelry. There was this girl Paula, who used to hang out with Tim and Randy and this guy Alan, and sometimes Beverly had gone wandering around stores with her. Not that they had been bosom buddies or anything. Paula was sort of a dolt.

She walked quickly past the library. She was sick of the library. Beyond it was Copley Square, which was just starting to get crowded again with the warm weather. During the sixties, it had probably been quite a beatnik hangout. Now, it was farmers markets, bag people, or religious types. Students too. There was this old church there, Trinity Church, and because the John Hancock Building was so heavy, the church was sinking, a few inches every year. Kind of a depressing thought. A metaphor, even, although the religious fanatics who shouted things through megaphones, standing in front of the church, had probably never thought of that.

The Public Gardens started at Arlington Street. Willow trees, flowers, a man-made pond. Tourists were always taking pictures of the swan-boats being pedaled around the pond, full of even more tourists. A Boston tradition. Oliver loved to ride on them.

She walked down one of the cement paths — you weren't supposed to walk on the grass, although lots of people did — and around the man-made pond once before sitting down on an empty bench, under a willow tree. Very peaceful. Most of the people walking in the park were either tourists, happy little families, or loving couples, but it didn't seem *too* bad to be alone. Other people were. No one really bothered anyone in the Public Gardens. Across the street, in the Boston Common, you could run into trouble maybe, but the Public Gardens were very quiet.

Since the flowers were just starting to come out, there were a lot of city workers around. Weeding, picking up trash, cutting the grass. Telling people to stay off it, probably. She opened her book.

One of the workers was fairly near her, emptying trash, and she wondered if she should move. While she was deciding, he saw her looking and grinned a crooked, arrogant grin. Oh, Christ, that was all she needed. She moved to another bench, away from him. He was a classic low-life: battered work shoes, old Levis, faded green, maybe too tight, T-shirt. Blondish hair, on the long side. Red Sox cap. A couple of years older, maybe more.

She tried to concentrate on her book, but couldn't help wondering if he were going to come over and say something mean. Or something sexual. You had to watch out in the city. Maybe she should just leave.

Except that there were a lot of people around, and damn it, she didn't feel like leaving. She had just gotten here. He would have to keep his distance — couldn't he lose his job for harassing people? Yeah, she was probably safe.

She glanced over and noticed that now he had his shirt off, tied casually around his waist, trying to show off his early tan or something. What a jerk. Why were guys like that? Did he think she was going to faint over his stupid muscles? What a total jerk.

She resumed her reading, but stiffened slightly, seeing out of the corner of her eyes that he was working his way closer. Major jerk. She would have to move again.

" 'Scuse me," he said, hefting the trash can closest to her onto his shoulders, the muscles in his back flexing.

Big wow. Hope you get a hernia. Beverly kept reading, or trying to, anyway.

He carried the can over to a City of Boston pickup truck, dumping the contents in and carrying it back.

He deposited it next to her bench and she could tell that he carefully wasn't out of breath.

"Good book?" he asked.

"It *was*," she said.

He shrugged an embarrassed, but cool, male shrug. " 'Scuse *me*," he said, and walked away. Swaggered, sort of.

Jerk. He was probably a rapist. Beverly hunched over her book, waiting to see if he were going to come back. If he did, she would leave. Of course, he could have just been being friendly. Friendly. Yeah, sure. Guys were all alike. When they were friendly, it was because they wanted something. Like she couldn't guess what *that* was.

He had a rake now, and was industriously raking the grass in her area, getting every scrap of trash. Still pretending to read, she moved to the edge of her bench, ready to leave. He was raking very hard, every muscle obvious.

Big deal, she said silently. So you have a good body. You want a medal or something?

"You come here a lot," he observed.

She sat up straight, scared now. Why was he talking to her? Maybe he was some kind of maniac. But she had to say something. "So what?" she asked in a "what's-it-to-you?" voice.

"Dunno. I was just saying." He raked still more industriously.

"Yeah, well, why don't you *quit* saying?"

He shrugged. "Dunno. Figured you were too pretty to be by yourself."

She slapped her book shut, standing up. "Screw you, buddy," she said in a low voice and walked swiftly away.

"Hey, wait!" He came after her, rake forgotten, grabbing her arm.

She jerked away, both scared and furious. "Touch me," she said, her voice shaking, "and I'll scream so loud the whole park'll hear."

He stared at her. "What's your problem? I wasn't going to do anything to you."

"Yeah," she nodded, "sure."

"Well, I wasn't."

"Bully for you." She hurried across the swan pond bridge, towards the exit of the park. Great, now even going to the *Public Gardens* was spoiled. What a jerk. One of the few places she actually enjoyed going, and now she wouldn't be able to anymore. At least, not without being nervous. It really wasn't fair. Why did guys have to be such jerks?

Chapter
Eight

But for some reason, even after she got home, she couldn't get the incident out of her head. Big wow. Some stupid, probably illiterate guy was halfway friendly. What was this, the highlight of her month? Her year? Like the saying went, how low could she go? From murderers to park psychopaths. Terrific. But she still kept thinking about it.

Her father and Maryanne wanted to go to a movie, so she stayed with Oliver, playing game after game of CandyLand. She despised CandyLand, but he was really into it. She put him to bed, read him *Horton Hears a Who*, then went into her own room to read. She shoved the unfinished Lurie into her bookcase, starting *Mansfield Park* instead. You were supposed to have read all that stuff before you went to college.

Oliver only woke up once, wanting orange juice, but she appeased him with a Cameo cookie instead.

They were supposed to avoid giving him liquids at night, since he was sort of at that age. She was glad she didn't have to deal with it. He was getting much better though.

Her father and stepmother came home around midnight, and while she couldn't hear exactly what they were saying, their inflections were relaxed and happy. In-love sounding. Had he and her mother ever sounded like that? They must have. She had only been in the third grade when they separated, so maybe she just couldn't remember — she bent over her book, not wanting to think about it.

Her father knocked and stuck his head in. "Is everything all right?"

"Yeah," she said. "He's been asleep since nine. How was the movie?"

"Not bad. Not wonderful." He yawned. "*Old Acquaintance* is on, if you want to watch it with us."

At least he was trying. She couldn't deny that. But, she would feel in the way, especially if they were being in-love and all. "No, thanks." She held up her book as evidence.

"See you in the morning, then."

"Yeah." She read for a while longer, then turned out the light. Another wild and crazy Saturday. And stupidly, the last thing she thought of before going to sleep, was the guy in the park. At least *someone* was friendly to her, someone her father wasn't paying. Oh, the novelty of it all. Christ. She sounded like Jane Muggins.

Sunday promised to be another long boring day. She slept late and when she got up, her father and Mary-anne were immersed in *The New York Times*. An all-day affair. And Oliver was going to a birthday party.

Unusually jittery, she went from her room, to the kitchen, even to the rocking chair in the living room.

"You want to make yourself useful," her father said, behind The Week in Review, "take Jason out."

"How far is he allowed to walk?" Lately, they had been cutting back on his distance.

"Oh, I don't know." Her father drank some coffee. "No further than the Public Gardens, say."

Beverly glanced at him. Maybe that was a sign, like that she really should go down there, maybe — "Okay."

"Can you pick up some milk on your way back?" Maryanne asked, reading the magazine section, and as Beverly nodded, her father took out his wallet, handing her five dollars.

Jason seemed to enjoy the first couple of blocks, pausing at his regular trees and street lights, but was more reluctant as they walked further.

"Come on," she said. "You're supposed to like this." But he moved listlessly, not even stretching the leash. She sighed. Smart dog. He knew when he was being used.

In the park, she paused, looking around. Because it was Sunday afternoon, it was pretty crowded, and she walked toward the bridge, seeing other, older workers. But then she located the boy — man? — mowing the grass near the main entrance, closer than she had anticipated. Today he was wearing a different T-shirt, faded navy, but that was about the only change. She stopped walking, feeling like an idiot. Talk about grasping at straws.

"You're right," she said to Jason. "This was a dumb idea." Well, she would just have to get out of here before he — damn it, damn it, damn it. What a moment for him to look up. Damn it. She turned to face

69

the other way, hoping that he hadn't recognized her. But the sound of the lawn mower was coming closer. *Damn it.*

She bent down to pretend to adjust Jason's collar, her face feeling hot. The lawn mower came even closer, then stopped.

"You forget something yesterday?" he asked.

Oh God, this was dumb. This was really dumb. "I'm walking my dog," she said stiffly. "Is there a law against that?"

He shrugged. "Dunno. Not on Sundays."

That was funny, and she considered smiling, but found herself blushing instead, wrapping Jason's leash tightly around her hand.

"I have to go," she said nervously.

"Who's stopping you?"

She clenched the leash, the chain links hurting her hand. "No one."

"So go already."

"I'm walking my dog," she said, stupidly, and did so, away from the boy, who really was a jerk apparently.

"Pretty dumb-looking mutt," he said after her.

Beverly spun around. "He's a schnauzer!"

" 'Scuse *me*," he said. "It's still dumb-looking."

Beverly bent to give Jason a protective pat.

"Doesn't mean it's not cute," the boy said.

"Oh, right. Dumb *and* cute?"

The boy grinned.

"I'm not stupid!" She said, feeling her cheeks flush.

"D'I say you were?"

"Yeah, well, I'm not cute either!"

He shrugged. " 'F you say so."

Completely embarrassed, she turned to leave, so

self-conscious that it was hard to walk naturally. He caught up to her with three long steps.

"Uh, look." He took off his Red Sox hat, frowned at the brim, put it back on. "I get off at five."

"Most people do," she said.

"Yeah, well, I kind of — I dunno, thought you — "

"Hey, Winters!" another worker yelled. "Let's move it!"

The boy glanced at him, then stuffed his hands into his pockets, not looking at her. "I gotta go."

She shrugged. "So go."

"Yeah."

"Get it in gear, Winters!" the supervisor said.

"Yeah, yeah, I'm coming." He looked at Beverly. "You, uh, coming here tomorrow?"

"Hey, look, pal," she said. "I just go where the dog wants to."

He studied her, his mouth twisting into an amused grimace. " 'F you say so," he said, and went back to his lawn mower.

She decided not to go back. Some stupid high school dropout, big deal. If she was going to spend her time lurking around the Public Gardens, she *really* had problems. So she came home from school on Monday — another lonely day — and paced around the apartment, sick of reading. She was so bored that she even sat in the kitchen and watched Maryanne brush Jason.

"When's Oliver going to get up?" she asked.

"Not any time soon, I hope," Maryanne said. "It took me over an hour to get him settled down."

Beverly sighed. She was bored enough to play Candy-Land even.

"You're pretty restless."

"No, I'm not," Beverly said.

"Sorry. My mistake." Her stepmother smiled at her. "Why don't you go out and get some fresh air? You'll feel better."

Beverly glanced at her. "You're telling me to go for a walk?"

Maryanne nodded. "Go burn off some energy."

Beverly thought about that. Well, see, it's not like I came down here on purpose — my stepmother *made* me. She jumped up. "Okay. See you later."

Maryanne looked startled. "Just like that?"

"Yeah." Beverly opened the front door. "Bye."

"Beverly — "

"Bye!" She closed the door, ran outside and down the front steps, then slowed to a walk, heading for the Public Gardens.

Except that he wasn't there. She looked all over the park, and he definitely wasn't there. She waited on the bridge, surprised by how disappointed she was, waiting around in case he had gone off to a men's room or something. But when he didn't show up after fifteen minutes, she gave up, the thought of returning home very depressing.

There were other workers around, so she decided to embarrass herself, walking up to two of them, her arms tight across her chest, making an effort not to blush.

"Uh, hi," she said to one of the men, who grinned. "I'm looking for one of the guys who works with you. His last name is Winters?"

"Derek, hunh?" The man grinned and winked at his friend, who also grinned.

Derek. Hunh. "Is he working today?" she asked, having to blush.

72

"Yeah," one said. "Over in the Common."

"Graveyard, I think," the other one contributed.

"Thank you." She hurried to the park exit, not looking back in case they were watching her.

The graveyard, an historical landmark, was by the Boylston subway station, across from the Colonial Theatre. He was in the far corner, weeding, and she took a minute to decide what to say. She couldn't come up with anything, so just walked over. From behind, he looked very tired.

She coughed. "Um, hi."

He turned, shoulders relaxing. "You again."

"You mean, *you* again. Don't you ever have days off?"

"Tuesdays. Every other weekend." He wiped his hands on his jeans. "Where's the dog?"

"He's old. He doesn't like to walk much."

"Oh yeah?"

"Yeah." She folded her arms, feeling like an idiot. Who was this guy? Just some jerky dropout. Why was she wasting her time like this?

"Leaving?" he asked.

"I guess so."

"Well, see ya." He turned back to the weeds.

"Yeah." She turned to leave. This time, she really wasn't coming back. Not ever. No more straw-grabbing.

"How's it look?"

She stopped. "What?"

"The graveyard. It look okay?"

She glanced around. It *did* look nice. The lawn neatly mowed, the grass around the headstones trimmed, almost all of the weeds gone.

"Been in here most of the day," he said.

73

"Well — it looks good." Pretty bland. "Very historic."

"Yeah? Think they had lawn mowers and everything?"

She flushed. Why was he making fun of her? He didn't even know her.

"That was a joke," he said.

"I know. Do you think I'm stupid or something?"

"Think you take things personally, is all." He straightened one tombstone, brushed off another. "You live around here?"

What a stupid question. "No. I walk up from Providence."

"No wonder your dog's tired."

"Yeah." This was so, so stupid. She started edging away.

"You go to school around here?"

She couldn't tell him the truth. If they ended up being friends, and he found out who she really was — there was no way he could live in Boston and not have heard about —

"Where you go?" he asked. "Winsor or someplace?"

Winsor was the best private girls' school in the city. She shrugged affirmatively.

"How come you're talking to me if you go to Winsor?"

"What do you mean?"

"I don't know." He gathered up the garden tools. "Don't guess I'm in your league."

"Well." She refolded her arms. "Maybe I'm not in any league."

"Free agent, hunh?"

She shrugged, looking at the grass.

"Why you wasting time on me?"

"What's *your* problem?"

"My problem?" He straightened up, taking a pack of Marlboros from his T-shirt pocket. "You smoke?"

She shrugged.

"Does that mean yes?"

She nodded and he handed her one, lighting it, then his own.

"Uh, thank you," she said.

"Y'owe me a nickel," he said.

She glanced up, startled.

"That was a joke."

"I know," she said defensively. "What, do you think I'm totally stupid?"

He looked at her, inhaling, then very slowly releasing the smoke. "Think you're totally *weird*," he said finally.

"Thanks a lot."

He grinned. "Don't mention it." He reached over to touch her, and she recoiled. "Uh, sorry." He pulled back, his expression both embarrassed and confused. "You like, have a problem with guys?"

"No!"

" 'F you say so." He walked over to the cast-iron fence, leaning against it, staring out at the street. "Can't figure what you want me to do."

"Who says I want you to do anything?"

"Well, I dunno," he said, turning around. "Seems like you keep getting mad."

"I'm not mad."

"Still can't figure what you want." He put his hands in his pockets, the cigarette hanging out of his mouth. "Like, if you weren't so totally weird, I'd ask you out." He frowned. "You'd prob'ly call the cops 'r something."

Beverly looked at him slouching against the fence, hair tousled, cigarette hanging. "Is this your James Dean imitation?"

"Give it more pain," he said, and slouched lower, demonstrating. He straightened. "So, do I ask you out, or what?"

"Couldn't we just be — friends or something?"

"Friends," he said.

"Well, yeah. I, uh," she coughed, "don't have so many right now."

"There something wrong with you?"

She tightened her arms, hunching over them.

"Sorry," he said. "That was mean." He took the cigarette out, studied it, then put it back in. "Actually," he exhaled, "I don't have so many myself."

"What's wrong with *you*?"

He shrugged. "Lots prob'ly. Anyway," he shifted his weight, "you don't seem like you'd be *too* bad of a friend."

Beverly also shrugged, her fists nervously tight. "Might not be that great."

Neither of them said anything.

"So, uh," he spoke first, "you doing anything tomorrow afternoon?"

"No, I — " Dr. Samuels. She sighed. "Yeah. I have a doctor's appointment."

He looked suspicious. "For real?"

"Oh, yeah," she said. "This is starting off great."

"Guess you really have a doctor's appointment."

She nodded.

"Well. You busy this weekend?"

"I don't think I can go out at night," she said uneasily.

"You turn into a werewolf?"

She shook her head.

"We could do something during the day." The part of his mouth without a cigarette grinned. "Hear friends do that sometimes."

She nodded.

"Can I call you? Like to — "

"No," she said quickly. "I mean — my father's strict."

"How strict?"

"Look, you want to meet here at one? On Saturday?"

He looked around the graveyard. *"Here?"*

"Why not?"

"Why not," he said.

"Okay." She took a first nervous puff of her cigarette. "Then, I'll — I'll see you then."

"Okay," he said, giving her a James Dean grin. "See ya."

She nodded, turning to leave.

"Hey, yo."

She paused.

"What's your name?" he asked.

Chapter
Nine

"So," Dr. Samuels said. "How was your week?"

"Splendid," she said. Derek's Marlboro had gotten her back in the mode and this time, she asked Dr. Samuels if she could have one of the Salem Lights from the desk drawer. "Your wife divorce you yet?"

"Not yet. Why was your week so splendid?"

"I don't know." She was tempted to knock her ashes onto his carpet, but used an ashtray instead. "Because life is such a special gift, I guess."

"Well, I'd have to agree with that," he said, but she could tell that he was amused. "What — "

"What makes it so special?" she asked, anticipating his question. What a boring guy.

"No," he said. "Actually, I was going to ask you what time it is."

She almost laughed, but managed not to.

"Really, how was your week?" he asked.

"I hardly know where to begin," she said.

"What did you do over the weekend?"

"The usual whirl of activities." She sighed. "Is it time to go yet?"

He shook his head.

"Christ." She slumped down in her chair. "Your wife must have a job that takes her out of town a lot."

He smiled, picking up his coffee mug. "How's school?"

"Oh, super."

"Looking forward to graduation?"

She frowned at him. "That's a stupid question."

"What do you mean?"

"Would *you* go to graduation if you were me?"

"I don't know," he said.

"Well, you wouldn't." She pulled over the pack of Salem Lights, lighting another.

"Why?"

She rolled her eyes, losing patience. "Are you really this stupid, or is it an act you pull to get people to talk?"

"I just want to be sure I understand," he said.

She moved her jaw. "Because I don't feel like being there when they get to Connors and say Considine instead. Because" — it was hard to say the name Colleen — "because, um, Colleen Spencer was going to be the valedictorian. What do you think they're all going to be thinking about when Matthew is giving his speech?"

He nodded.

"And Christ, with *me* sitting there, they'd really — I mean, they all — " She frowned. Was he trying to trick her into talking?

"They all what?"

She didn't answer, concentrating on her cigarette.

He waited briefly, then sat back. "What was she like?"

"Who, Colleen?"

He nodded.

"Well — " As questions went, that one was probably harmless enough. "I don't know. Smart."

He nodded.

"Really popular, really pretty — you know."

He nodded.

"She was kind of funny too. Like, she hated gym, so she was always showing up with canes and eye-patches and slings and all." Beverly smiled a little, remembering Colleen refusing to get on the balance beam on the grounds that she suffered from vertigo, and when the teacher made her, she'd requested smelling salts. "I don't know." Beverly frowned, almost forgetting where she was. "It always seemed funny that she didn't have more friends."

Dr. Samuels raised his eyebrows.

"I mean, yeah, pretty much everyone liked her, but she didn't seem like she had a lot of *friends*. Mostly she hung out with Patrick Finnegan." Beverly shifted in the chair, not enjoying remembering any of this.

"What about Susan?"

"Well, she — " Beverly bit her lip, hearing Susan's very quiet, "All you had to do was *tell* someone."

"Beverly?"

She scowled at him. "I guess they were good friends, but Susan had moved away, okay? Christ."

"Were *you* and Colleen friends?"

"Right."

"Why?"

"Don't you get it at all?" she asked. "I've never really been *friends* with anyone." Not since elementary school,

80

anyway. "And don't, for God's sakes, ask me why."

"*Is* there a reason?"

"Because I want people to leave me the hell alone, okay? Jesus!"

"Beverly — "

"Just leave me alone," she said, turning in her chair so she wouldn't be facing him. "Please, just leave me alone."

Her week didn't exactly go uphill from there and by Saturday morning, she was a nervous wreck. The thought of having to hang out with someone for an afternoon was terrifying; the thought that he might not show up was even worse.

"You have any plans today?" Maryanne asked, sitting at the kitchen table, writing on a legal pad when Beverly came in to get some orange juice.

"Plans?" Beverly asked, trying not to sound guilty. "Uh, not really. The library, I guess."

"Well, we're never going to get your father away from the game, but I thought that maybe you and Oliver and I could — "

"Um, I have a lot of work to do," Beverly said.

"Oh. Well, okay." Maryanne scanned the three books open in front of her, and went back to writing.

"It's nothing personal," Beverly said, feeling guiltier. She'd spent the last three years refusing to go places. "I just — because the library's open today and — "

"It's really all right," Maryanne said.

"Yeah, but I don't want you to think — " Beverly blushed. Since when did she go around apologizing to Maryanne? Very red, she finished pouring her juice and put the carton away.

"Why don't you have a bagel or something too?"

Not wanting to cause trouble, Beverly got herself a bagel from the brown paper bag in the refrigerator.

"And some cream cheese," Maryanne said.

Beverly looked up uneasily and saw her stepmother's grin.

"Chop up some olives too," Maryanne said.

Beverly took a bite out of the bagel without even cutting it.

"Then again," Maryanne said. "You could just have it plain."

Beverly opened the refrigerator, lifting out the butter dish. Margarine, actually, so her father wouldn't eat too much cholesterol. She cut the bagel in half, neatly spreading margarine on each side.

"Then again," Maryanne said, and went back to writing.

By twelve-thirty, Beverly was even more nervous. She tried on a couple of different outfits, ending up with well broken-in jeans, but a very nice pale blue sweater. She put on just enough perfume for her father not to notice, grabbed a couple of notebooks and went down to the living room where he was correcting papers, Oliver sitting next to him on the couch and telling some long, involved story.

"I'm going to the library," she said.

Her father looked up, then frowned. "That's what you wear to the library?"

"*Jeans?*" she asked, purposely misunderstanding. "What, I have to dress up?"

He was still frowning. "When will you be back?"

"I don't know. Dinnertime?"

He checked his watch. "You don't have that much to do. I want you back by three."

"Yeah, but — " Protesting would make him more suspicious. "I have a lot of work to do, Dad."

"Not *that* much."

"Yeah, but — " She sighed. In the old days, she would have yelled that he didn't have any power over her and stormed out of the house, but these days — well, he had power over her.

"What's going on?" Maryanne asked, in the kitchen doorway, her eyes on Beverly's father.

"Everything's under control," he said stiffly.

"*Strict* control," Maryanne said.

"For once, stay out of it, okay? She's *my* daughter!"

Maryanne started to say something, looked at Beverly, and stopped. "Fine," she said and went back into the kitchen, Beverly hearing a cupboard door slam open harder than necessary.

"Is Mommy mad?" Oliver asked, sounding worried.

"No, don't worry, everything's fine," Beverly's father said, giving him a reassuring smile. He looked at Beverly, the smile fading. "Four-thirty," he said grimly. "Not one minute later."

She nodded, opening the front door.

"Hey, wait!" Oliver scrambled off the couch after her. "Can I come too? Can I?"

"Not this time," Beverly said. "I'll do something with you tomorrow, okay?"

"Will you play when you get home?"

She nodded.

"CandyLand?"

She nodded.

Finally outside, she sat on the front steps for a minute. Just barely out of the apartment, and she was already tired. Maybe she *should* just go to the library. Except that it was getting close to one, and if she was

83

late, he might leave. If he had come at all, that is.

She walked as quickly as she could, not slowing until she was actually in the Common. What if he wasn't there? There was a good chance that he might not have come. Maybe he — she could see someone in the cemetery as she walked closer. Jeans, jeans jacket. She saw the Red Sox cap and cigarette, and relaxed.

"So," he said. "You came."

"So did you."

He nodded. "Looks that way."

There was a brief silence.

"I-I have to be home by four-thirty," she said.

"Guess that means we can't leave the state."

Don't overreact — that's his sense of humor. "You think you're a pretty funny guy, don't you," she said.

Derek grinned. "Kind of."

"I figured," she said, nodding.

"What, you don't think I'm funny? Most chicks do."

"*Chicks?*" she said.

He shrugged. "Chicks, broads, dames."

"You really call women 'broads'?"

He shrugged. "When I'm being polite."

Beverly stared at him, hands moving to her hips. "That's terrible."

He shrugged again. "You, you're more of a skirt."

"A *skirt?*"

"A gullible skirt."

Got her again. Embarrassed, she kicked at the grass with one moccasin.

"Watch it," he said. "People work hard planting that stuff."

She stopped kicking.

"I was kidding," he said. "You weren't hurting it."

Completely self-conscious, she folded her arms.

"You wanna go get something to eat?"

She looked up. "Eat?"

"I don't know," he said, then grinned. "Friends say one — I figure lunch."

"You figure lunch," she said, having to grin herself.

"Absolutely." He moved his arm as though he were going to drape it around her, hesitated, and put his hands in his pockets. "C'mon."

They walked out of the cemetery, a few awkward feet apart.

"I'm not a rich guy," he said, very defensive. "Can't take you to the kind of place you're prob'ly used to."

"Who says I'm used to a particular kind of place?"

"Dunno," he said. "Just figured."

"Well, that's pretty stupid."

" 'Scuse *me*." He jammed his hands further into his pockets.

"Well, it is."

"I dunno," he said, still defensive. "You mind McDonald's?"

She stopped. "If you're going to act like this, I'm going home."

"So go."

"You wouldn't care?"

He shrugged.

"Fine," she said. "Have a nice lunch." She strode away, feeling more shaky than angry. What a jerk. What a completely stupid jerk.

"Hey, wait! You leaving?"

She walked faster.

"Beverly, wait!" He ran after her. "I didn't mean it."

She turned, arms wrapped around herself even though it wasn't cold.

"I'm sorry," he said, quietly.

"Just don't yell at me," she said, also quiet. "Okay?"

"I wasn't. I just — " He slouched against a tree. "You make me nervous, is all."

"I make *you* nervous?"

He nodded and they didn't say anything, Derek slouching, Beverly studying a piece of gum someone had dropped.

"Oh, hell," he said. "Let's start over." He straightened. "How about we get something to eat?"

She nodded.

"McDonald's okay?"

She nodded.

There was one on Boylston Street and going in, Derek held the door for her.

"What do you want?" he asked.

"Um, just a medium 7-Up."

He frowned. "You got one of those diet diseases?"

"N-no. I just — well, I had a bagel before."

"Oooh," he said. "Blimp City."

She flushed.

"You get us a table, and I'll surprise you."

She pulled a few dollars out of her pocket.

"This one's on me," he said.

"No, I — "

"Friends can do that," he said, walking up to the front counter.

She was going to protest, but it would be too embarrassing to shout after him, so she looked around for a table. There was an empty booth on one side and she sat down in it, folding her hands in her lap.

He carried over a tray with soda, two coffees, a Big Mac, a Quarter Pounder, a hamburger, a cheeseburger, and two large orders of french fries.

"Is someone else joining us?" she asked.

He grinned, sitting down. "Thought you might want a choice."

"Seems like kind of a waste."

"Don't worry, I'll eat what's leftover." He studied the tray. "Can prob'ly eat twice this much."

She also looked at the tray. "That's disgusting."

He just grinned, opening the two coffees, dumping half a packet of sugar in each. Beverly took her 7-Up and the small hamburger.

"Not even the cheeseburger?" he asked.

"I had a bagel before."

He switched the hamburger for the cheeseburger.

"Derek, I really don't — "

"What the hell," he said. "Walk on the wild side."

She glanced up. "You like Lou Reed?"

"Sure," he said. "Why not."

He was eating the Big Mac, so she opened her cheeseburger, taking a small bite.

"You sure you don't have a diet problem?" he asked.

She nodded.

"Must have been one hell of a big bagel."

She nodded. She couldn't think of anything to say, so she sipped her soda and he drank some coffee.

"Want some french fries?" he asked.

"Um, a couple maybe."

He shook some onto her cheeseburger wrapper, she nodded thank you, and he nodded back.

"Catsup?" he asked.

"No. Thank you."

He nodded, picking up his Big Mac, and she ate one of the french fries.

"Can't figure what to talk about," he said.

She couldn't either, so she took a napkin from the tray, spreading it on her lap.

"Don't guess we have a whole lot in common," he said.

"I guess not."

He folded his arms, leaning forward on them to look at her. "Bet you're the smart kid in class and that's why you hang out alone so much."

She shook her head.

"Bullshit, you're not smart." He indicated the notebooks. "Why else would you carry those around?"

"My poetry," she said grimly.

"You, uh, you write poetry?"

She shook her head.

"That's good," he said, opening the Quarter Pounder. "I prob'ly wouldn't have appreciated it."

She laughed.

"Decided I'm funny?"

"Yeah," she said.

As he ate, she noticed how brown his hands and wrists were. From being outdoors so much, probably. Except that he had looked pretty brown that day he was walking around with his shirt off. Tans like that took effort.

"How come you have such a good tan already?"

He stopped chewing. "Y'haven't heard?"

She shook her head.

"Chicks really go for tans."

"Oh, they do, hunh?"

"Absolutely," he said, and winked at her.

"Not impressed," she said.

"And here I was," his voice was sad, "thinking you were. Bet you go for guys who like chemistry and wear glasses and stuff."

She shook her head, one fist involuntarily tightening as she thought about Tim. Big, blond, and arrogant. Like Derek. Oh, God. She gripped the side of the table, feeling such a wave of fear that she was dizzy. What if it was a pattern? Big, tough guys who —

"You okay?" he asked, his hand tentatively coming over to cover hers.

She stared at it, then up at him, aware that she was trembling. The eyes were different. Tim's were always cool and superior. Cynical. Very light, more grey than blue. Derek's were much brighter, with maybe a greenish tint. Kinder too. Tim's eyes had never been kind. Surely her judgment couldn't be that bad *twice*. Except that she didn't know anything about this guy and maybe —

"What is it?" he asked.

The voice was gentle too. But maybe Tim had sounded gentle, at least when he wanted — "I, uh — " She swallowed. "I have an ulcer," she said finally. "It hurts sometimes."

"Are you okay?" he asked, sounding nervous. "Should I get you some milk?"

"I'm fine," she said.

"Yeah, but — will you have an attack?"

"I'm fine," she said, picking up her cheeseburger to prove it.

"How'd you get it?"

She sighed. "Jordan Marsh was having a sale."

"What are you, seventeen? Isn't that kind of young to be getting ulcers?"

She pressed her molars together. "Probably."

"Well, I mean, should I — "

"Nice weather we're having," she interrupted, "don't you think?"

"Uh, yeah," he said. "Real nice."

89

Chapter Ten

The conversation was pretty awkward after that. Even *more* awkward.

"How about a milkshake?" he asked, the food finished.

"Derek, I'm fine."

"I buy it, you have to eat it," he said and got up, returning with a chocolate one and a vanilla. "Have one."

She sighed and pulled over the vanilla shake.

"Yup," he said. "Knew you'd pick that."

"Do you want it?"

"Hell, no." He took out his cigarettes, lifted an eyebrow at her, and she nodded. He lit two, handing her one.

"Bet chicks really go for that," she said.

He grinned. "You know it."

For some reason, the milkshake tasted very good.

"Want a couple more?" he asked.

She blushed and shook her head.

"Okay, then." He smiled at her. "Let's travel."

"San Francisco's nice," she said.

"Thought you had to be home by four-thirty."

"Yeah." She looked at the clock up behind the front counter. Two-fifteen. Two hours. What were they going to do for two hours?

"So," he said, holding the door for her. "What do friends do after lunch?"

She shrugged uneasily.

"Prob'ly be stupid to go get something to eat."

She nodded.

"Most afternoons, you prob'ly go to museums."

She shook her head.

"What *do* you do?"

What *did* she do? She shrugged.

"You're like, real good with words," he said.

"Um, yeah," she said.

"Always thought that like, the *boy* was supposed to be the shy one."

"Um, yeah." She had to say *something*. "Do you, um, have any brothers and sisters?"

"A brother. He's in the Navy."

"What's his name?"

"Sam."

"Where's he stationed?"

"Pensacola."

They both nodded.

It seemed more natural to walk now, and they headed up Boylston Street.

"What about you?" he asked.

"Um, a half-brother," she said. "He's five."

Derek nodded, and they crossed Arlington Street.

"Where'd you tell your father you were going today?"

"The library." She indicated the notebooks.

"Good," he said. "That means it isn't poetry."

"No," she agreed. "Philosophical essays, mostly."

His smile was only a little uncertain. "Don't guess your father would approve of me, hunh?"

"No," she said quickly. "It doesn't have anything to do with you. He's just — strict."

Derek started to say something, but stopped. "What's he do?" he asked finally. "For a job, I mean."

"He's a professor."

"Harvard, prob'ly."

Beverly blushed, but nodded.

"No shit?" Derek shoved his hands into his pockets. "Guess he *really* wouldn't approve of me then."

"Why?"

"I'm not exactly Joe College."

More like Joe Street Punk. She wanted to ask if he was a dropout, but that seemed kind of rude. No matter how curious she was. Maybe if she phrased it — "Um, where'd you go to school?"

"Boston-English," he said. "Graduated last June."

She wanted to ask why he hadn't gone to college, but that would be obnoxious. Not *everyone* automatically went to college. "So, you're nineteen," she said.

"Yeah." He glanced over. "You're what — a senior?"

She nodded.

"Guess you're going away to college and all in September."

She hesitated, but nodded.

"Suppose you're going to some really good school," he said.

"Um, Wesleyan."

"Where's that, Connecticut or something?"

She nodded.

"You looking forward to it?"

"I guess so."

"My family's not much for college," he said.

She nodded, hating herself for feeling like a well-meaning white-collar liberal.

"Doesn't mean I'm stupid," he said, sounding more defensive. "Just never liked school much."

She shrugged. "Lots of people don't."

"You've just never met one."

To her horror, she blushed. "Of course I have."

"Oh, yeah. Lots." His shoulders hunched a little. "My brother's having an okay time. Gets to go lots of places and everything. Figured I might do that, or join the Army."

She nodded, feeling as if she were doing so too vigorously.

"Prob'ly sounds weird to you."

"People should do what they want," she said.

"Well, don't guess I'll ever go to college."

She shrugged her liberal shrug.

"You embarrassed to be seen with me?"

"No."

"Just too embarrassed to tell your father."

"Derek — " She stopped and looked at him. "It has nothing to do with you, okay? It's just — a situation."

"Well." His hands went further into his pockets. "Don't guess I'm one to pry."

She nodded, relieved, and they kept walking.

"D'ja get pregnant?" he asked.

"Derek!"

"Sorry," he said. He looked over. "You get a B in a class maybe?"

She sighed. "No."

"You never got a B in a class?"

"No, I — " She stopped. "Look, can we drop it?"

" 'F you say so."

They walked without speaking.

"I guess," she sighed, "it does seem weird that you would want to go join the Army or something."

"Doesn't bother me long as you admit it," he said, then tilted his head to look at her. "How come it seems weird?"

"It's not that someone would *want* to do it, but — I don't know. You don't seem the type."

He shrugged. "Not much future in what I'm doing now."

"Yeah, but — " She frowned. "I don't know. I don't see you taking orders from people. And what if you had to fight?"

"I don't know," he said, his shrug more unhappy. He pointed at a store up the street. "You want to go look at records or something?"

"Sure," she said.

They walked in, both hesitating near the front of the store. Beverly looked at him and decided to move first, going over to the Folk and Country section, flipping through albums by the Judds in great fascination. He didn't follow her, and she turned around, locating him at the Opera section, just as mesmerized. She walked over behind him, sure that he knew she was there, and heard him sing "O sole mio", making his voice a surprisingly good, deep vibrato.

"Trained voice, hunh?" she said, and grinned

He nodded, singing *"Mio, mio sole."*

"You're very good," she said.

"Kind of," he agreed, reading the back of a Placido Domingo record.

"Maybe you're funny after all," she said.

"Maybe you are too," he said.

He put the album down and they walked over to the Rock and Roll section.

After hanging around in the record store, they wandered up Boylston Street, drifting in and out of stores.

"Think I need ice cream," Derek said as they passed a Brigham's.

"You're going to eat *again*?" she asked.

"I'm hungry."

"You ever been checked for worms?"

He laughed and went inside, returning with a two-scoop cone. Chocolate and chocolate chip.

"What a pig," she said.

"Sure you don't want some?"

She nodded. There was something too romantic about sharing an ice cream cone.

"You live near here?" he asked. "It's going on to four."

"Yeah, on Marlborough."

" 'M I going to be allowed to walk you home?" He grinned. "Just like, to make sure you make it okay."

"I'll be fine."

"Yeah, but I'd like to — "

"Really," she said, "I'll be fine."

"Whatever." He shifted his weight. "Can I call you or anything?"

"My father — "

"Yeah, your father," he said.

"I can't help it."

He shrugged, eating his ice cream cone.

"Are you mad?" she asked uneasily.

"I don't know. Prob'ly not." He sighed. " 'M I ever going to see you again, or what?"

"Do you ever *want* to?"

"What the hell," he said, then let out his breath. "Don't guess your father would believe the library on a Sunday."

"No," Beverly agreed. "Anyway," she gestured toward his Red Sox cap, "you can watch the game."

"Hey, yo," he said, "you like baseball?"

"Well — " She grinned sheepishly. "I don't know. It's okay."

He also grinned. "You're more of a Bruins fan."

"Yeah," she said, to save time.

"So, you busy Tuesday?"

"Uh, yeah," she said.

"Let me guess. Doctor's appointment."

She flushed.

"What, you have one every week? What kind of — " He stopped, looking guilty. "Oh."

"It's not that big a deal," she said.

He nodded the same way she must have when he said he might join the Army.

"Derek — "

"You know," he said, "you come by around three-thirty, afternoons, I can take my break then."

"Any afternoons?"

"Absolutely."

"Well." She smiled shyly. "Maybe I will."

He insisted on walking her to the corner of Marlborough and Exeter, just like, to make sure she made it safely; Beverly worrying every step of the way that they might run into her father walking Jason. But they didn't, and it was only four-fifteen, so she made it home with time to spare.

"I'm back," she said loudly.

Her father grunted, watching the Red Sox wrap-up.

"I mean, I'm home in time."

He nodded, frowning at the television.

"Well." She hugged her notebooks closer, kind of deflated by the lack of response. "Did they win?"

"No," he said, frowning. "Damned Orioles." He leaned forward to turn off the set. "Did you finish your work?"

"Mostly."

"Good." He took off his glasses, rubbing the bridge of his nose. "Maryanne and Oliver went up to the garden. They should be back soon."

Beverly nodded.

"Well, then," he said and put his glasses back on.

Beverly couldn't think of anything to say, so she edged toward the stairs and her room.

"Your exams must be approaching," he said.

"Um, yeah. Pretty soon."

"And you expect to do well."

She nodded.

"Good," he said, and reached for a book. End of conversation.

"Dad?"

He looked up.

"What am I going to do this summer?"

He frowned. "In what sense?"

"I don't know. Can I at least get a job or something?"

He nodded. "That would be a good idea." He opened his book. "I'm sure I can find something at the university for you."

"I can't just — I don't know — work at a McDonald's or something?"

"I'd prefer your being at the university."

Working in his department, no doubt. But better than nothing at all. "Okay," she said.

"Then I'll look into it."

She nodded, starting up the stairs.

"Would you mind watching Oliver for a few hours tonight, and maybe making some dinner for the two of you? The Walshes invited us for cocktails."

She shrugged affirmatively.

"Good," he said.

Chapter
Eleven

All anyone at school talked about was the prom. Like, big deal. She and Randy had gone to the Junior Prom; Tim had taken this incredibly beautiful and incredibly vacuous girl named Priscilla. Randy had worn a pale blue tux. Jesus. They had all gotten pretty coked up, and Beverly couldn't really remember the parties they went to after, except that they weren't much fun. She had gone to a lot of parties like that with Tim — dark rooms thick with marijuana smoke, the Grateful Dead or Pink Floyd blasting. And a bunch of completely blown-away people, half of them passing out or getting sick from drinking too much, the rest making out all over the place. They'd been kind of boring. What she remembered.

In the locker room before gym, the endless prom conversations went on around her — who was going with whom, what everyone was going to wear, if Angela was going to be able to get a date. Talk about boring. Beverly changed quickly, almost looking forward to getting out to the gym and playing badminton.

"So, who are *you* going with?" Edith Patterson asked, her voice extra-loud.

Beverly knew without looking up that the question was directed at her, and concentrated on tying her sneaker to keep from telling her to fuck off. Edith had been her tenth grade biology lab partner. Beverly had always done all of the work.

"No one asked you, hunh?" Edith said, a few people laughing nervously, the others watching.

Beverly tied her other shoe.

"Maybe if the Parole Board meets in time, you can get a date."

It was very quiet, everyone waiting to see what would happen, and Beverly swallowed, not sure if she was going to cry, or just run out. She glanced across the locker room at Susan, who looked away guiltily, suddenly very busy with something inside her locker.

"No one wants you there anyway," Edith said. "You'd just — "

"Okay, girls," their teacher, Miss Jenkins, said, coming out of her office. "Let's hustle."

Beverly jumped up, making it out to the gym first, her back feeling very exposed. She stood by the bleachers, wanting to hide underneath them as the others came noisily out. But then she pictured Colleen, lying on the bleachers once, clutching her side, saying, "Dear God, it's the Spencer gallbladder." Even Miss Jenkins had laughed that time. Beverly closed her eyes, moving away from the bleachers.

Miss Jenkins blew her whistle. "Come on, girls, get some games going!"

Beverly watched people choose partners, taking badminton rackets and shuttlecocks from the pile by the stack of gymnastics mats. Jane Muggins looked at her and she nodded, going over to get a racket. What was she going to do if Jane was absent someday?

It seemed overeager to go down and see Derek right away, so she waited until Wednesday afternoon, telling Maryanne that she was going for a walk. Maryanne, who was pretty busy working on her thesis these days, nodded almost without looking up from her legal pads, obviously trying to finish something before it was time for Oliver to get up from his nap.

It was exactly three-thirty when she got to the Public Gardens. He was cutting the grass over in the Beacon Street side of the park, wearing a maroon T-shirt, his cap down low over his eyes. She walked over, waving when he looked up, and he turned off the lawn mower, grinning and pushing his cap back.

"Was kind of figuring you'd come on Monday," he said.

"Well, I thought — I mean — " She blushed. "I don't know. I thought it might be pushy."

"Well, I was kind of disappointed and stuff." He turned toward some other workers near the supply shed. "Yo, Mitch! Taking my break now!"

One of the men nodded and Derek turned back.

"So," he said, and took his cigarettes out of his T-shirt pocket. "Want one?"

"Yeah."

They sat on a bench near the street.

"How you doing?" he asked.

"Okay. How are you?"

"Not bad."

101

They sat and smoked, Beverly with her leg crossed over her knee, Derek slouched down with his ankles crossed, arms stretched out along the side of the bench.

"Keep thinking it'll get easier," he said.

"Easier?"

"Talking to you and stuff. But — I don't know."

She looked at him, noticing how strange it was to see someone so big, so nervous. Very cool, but still pretty obviously nervous.

"What's your life like?" she asked.

"My *what*?"

"Your life. I mean," her face felt warmer, "what do you do? Where do you live. That kind of stuff."

"Hunh," he said, then grinned. "Grew up in a small mining town in Pennsylvania."

Was that Derek humor? Sounded like it. "So did I," she said.

"Hey, yo. Guess we have more in common than I thought." He looked at her, eyes amused. "D'ja mine coal or iron?"

"Diamonds," she said. "Up in the Poconos."

"I'll be damned." He lifted his hand as though he were going to touch her hair, but let it fall back on the bench. "We were copper people."

She smiled. "What's your life like really?"

"I don't know. Not too interesting."

"I'm interested," she said. "Where do you live?"

"South End."

"Do you have an apartment?"

"It's more like a cave," he said.

"I meant, do you have an apartment, or do you live with your family?"

"My family. It's not like I'm scared to move out'r anything, I just — " He looked at his watch.

"Do you have to go?"

He shook his head.

"With your brother gone, they must have lots of room."

"Kind of," he said briefly.

Silence. Unable to think of another conversational gambit, Beverly concentrated on what was left of her cigarette.

"See," Derek said, "the thing is, my father's not real reliable. It's not that he's not — well, he's not so great about money."

Beverly nodded.

"I don't know. Sam prob'ly had the right idea — joining up and stuff. But, I figured — " He looked at her uncertainly. "This is, like, really boring."

"No, it isn't."

"Well, I got the job here and I just figured that — well, instead of moving and all, I could give my mother money, tell my father it was like me paying rent, and then my mother wouldn't have to worry so much about bills."

"Hunh," Beverly said, impressed. He *was* a nice guy.

"Old Sammy never got along so great with my father. I always figured he'd take off soon as he was old enough." Derek stubbed his cigarette out on the side of the bench, very slowly. "Tried a couple times when he was younger, but the cops — " He sighed. "Hell, I don't know."

"It sounds like he took off and left you with all the responsibility."

Derek glanced over. "Wouldn't of figured you to be much of a listener."

"Of course I listen," she said, offended.

"Guess I didn't figure your hearing'd be so good."

"What's your father like?"

"He's an okay guy. Not really there when you need him, but at least he feels bad about it."

Beverly nodded.

"It's not that he's not — I mean — "

"Hey, Derek!" A man — his supervisor, probably — called, tapping his watch with one hand.

Derek nodded back, putting his cigarette out, then leaning over to drop it into a garbage can.

"Back to work," Beverly said.

"Yeah."

They stood up, not really looking at each other.

"Y'coming back anytime soon?" he asked.

"Um, is tomorrow okay?"

He grinned. "Yeah."

Except for Tuesday — and Sunday, when she couldn't think of an excuse, since the library was closed — she went every day. Finals were so close that neither her father nor Maryanne were suspicious.

"Guess you still say you're going to the library," Derek said on Monday, indicating her knapsack.

"I *do* go," she said. "Finals start next week."

He grinned. "We going to see a nice card of A's?"

She also grinned, but wryly. "If not, they're going to be pretty suspicious, what with all this time at the library."

"Sure would make it easier if you'd tell them the truth."

"If I tell them the truth, you'll never see me again."

"What, I'm so bad a guy they wouldn't — "

She closed her eyes. He had to stop pushing her. She couldn't be friends with him if he kept pushing her. "Don't keep doing this, okay? Please?"

"Yeah, yeah, I know." He sighed. "Just wish I could see you more, is all."

She glanced over nervously — that was a *boy*friend remark.

"It's nice to spend time with a friend," he said, with such an innocent little-boy expression that she forgot to be tense.

"You're such a jerk," she said, trying not to smile.

"Because I want to be with my friend?" he asked sadly.

"What a total jerk."

He grinned, lighting two cigarettes and handing her one.

"Chicks really go for that," she said.

"Yup, you know it." He looked across the park and sighed. "Oh, hell."

Beverly followed his gaze and saw his supervisor motioning him over. Twenty minutes sure went fast.

"How long you stay at the library?" he asked.

She shrugged. "Four-thirty, five."

"How about I meet you there a couple minutes after five?"

"But I have to go right home."

"So I'll walk you."

"Yeah, but — "

"Gotta go," he said. "See you out in front."

"Um, okay," she said.

She was sure that they were going to run into her father coming home — and almost hoped they would, just to get it over with. But her block was pretty quiet.

"Looks like you're safe," Derek said.

"Yeah."

" 'Course," he sat down on the brownstone steps, "I could always wait."

Remembering Derek humor, she managed not to overreact. "I'll deny everything."

"Think he'd beat me up?"

She smiled, picturing her father involved in what he would no doubt describe as "fisticuffs." "Probably not."

"Don't guess I'll risk it though." He stood up. "See you Wednesday?"

She nodded.

Inside, Maryanne and Oliver were watching Mister Rogers talk about how nice fish were.

"Can we get some fish, Mommy?" Oliver was asking.

Fish. Oliver asked for a different pet almost every day. Beverly figured Maryanne would get him a cat — as soon as she could persuade Beverly's father that Jason's psyche wouldn't be damaged by this. "Uh, hi," she said, closing the front door.

"Beverly, guess what!" Oliver said. "We're getting fish!"

"Well, I don't know," Maryanne said. "I thought some ferrets would be nice."

"Um, yeah," Beverly said, heading for her room. Weird.

"How was the library?" Maryanne asked.

"Fine."

"Stir-fry sound okay for dinner?"

"Whatever." Beverly shifted her weight, anxious to leave.

"Do you have more studying to do?"

Good, an exit. "Yeah, lots. I'll be in my room if anyone wants me."

Maryanne nodded, and she left.

"What was it like living with your mother?" Dr. Samuels asked.

She shrugged. "Quiet."

"So, it changed when your father left?"

She had to smile, trying to imagine someone describing her father as "noisy."

"What?" Dr. Samuels asked.

"I don't know. My father isn't exactly rowdy, you know?"

"So, how was it quiet?"

"Well — I don't know." She stopped smiling. "I guess my mother got quiet. I mean, especially after we left Hanover, and — " She shook her head. "I thought you weren't going to pressure me."

"Just trying to get a clearer picture of things," he said.

"Christ."

"Just give it a try."

"For Christ's sakes." She saw that he wasn't going to let her off the hook, and folded her arms. "They got divorced. He got a chair at Harvard and moved. We moved to Manchester."

"Why?"

"How the hell am I supposed to know? I was little."

"Why do you think your mother got quiet?"

"Why do you *think?* Mom — " She tried not to stutter over the word, clenching her fist so she wouldn't cry saying it — "I guess she felt funny with people she knew because everyone else was all tied up with the university, and she wasn't anymore. I mean — if he hadn't moved to Boston, we probably would have. Sh-she really liked cities. So, Manchester was kind of like one."

"What then?" he asked when she didn't go on.

"I don't know," Beverly said, defensively. "She was sad. Her mother died, she couldn't get a good job

107

because she hadn't been able to finish her degree before she and my father — I mean, she went to a school in Manchester, but she didn't really like it, or — I don't know."

"Where was she working?"

"I don't know. She didn't really like — I mean, different places. Like, an office supply house. A real estate office. A place where they did data processing. I mean, she wanted to teach, but to do that, she had to finish — " Beverly stopped, remembering night after night of finding her mother sitting alone, a book open on her lap, not turning pages. "Then, um, when my father got married again, she felt *really* bad."

"How soon after the divorce was that?"

"Well — " Beverly frowned at him. "I mean, not *that* soon. He didn't even meet her for a couple of years. I mean — she may not be my favorite person in the world, but she's not *that* much of a jerk."

Dr. Samuels nodded. "Why, particularly, did your mother feel so badly?"

"Well — why else? Because Maryanne was so young and all. She thought my father was being a real — I mean, she hadn't met anyone she liked, so she felt — " Beverly stopped again. "I wasn't supposed to tell my father. I mean, she didn't want him to know that she felt so — " She stopped again. She should have told someone. The goddamn story of her life.

"Well," Dr. Samuels said, "maybe — "

"I'm not talking about it anymore," Beverly said, tightening her arms across her stomach.

"Do you think what happened to her has anything to do with things that have happened since?"

"Boy," she said, "you must have majored in psychology."

"Did you ever wonder why you have an ulcer?"

She scowled, moving her hand away from her stomach. "It can be hereditary." Not that she knew of any relative who had one.

"Maybe you have a tendency to internalize."

"Gosh, I don't know," she said. Talk about understatements. "Maybe."

"Maybe here would be a good place for you to practice opening up."

She shrugged.

"Think how much better you feel when you have a nightmare, and you tell someone about it," he said.

She frowned. "I don't *ever* tell people my nightmares."

"It can make it easier to — "

"Oh, yeah, right," she said. "Like I'm going to tell *you*. You'll think they're all about sex or something."

"Are they?"

"No," she said, impatiently. "They're just like — they're blatant. Tim trying to get me, Susan and Colleen there, maybe. Or other people from school. Or like, I don't know, seeing my mother somewhere and she doesn't know who I am — I mean, *Christ*. It's not like that's hard to figure out."

"What do you think they mean?"

"Gosh, I don't know," she said. "Must be I'm tense."

He nodded. "How do you feel when you wake up?"

"Like killing myself," she said without thinking, "how else?"

He nodded.

"Oh, Christ, now you're going to call my father and tell him, right?"

He shook his head.

"It's not like I'm going to *do* it," she said. "I think

109

it really *sucks* when — " She stopped. Damn it, damn it, damn it. She was saying too much. "I mean, Christ, the most I'd do would be live dangerously, or — " Terrific. Open mouth, insert other foot. She sat back, folding her arms.

"Beverly — "

"I *really* don't want to talk about it," she said.

"Well, maybe — "

"Look," she interrupted, "if you want to know stuff, why don't you just ask my father? You guys talk about everything that goes on here, right?"

"I think you know we don't," he said.

"Oh, yeah, right," she said. "I bet he's on the phone every Wednesday morning."

He looked at her thoughtfully. "A lot of people have let you down, haven't they? People you've trusted."

"Oh, yeah," she said. "All those people."

"Tim. Your mother. Your father."

"What exactly is it that my father did?" she asked stiffly.

"He didn't understand."

"Oh?" She clenched her fists under her folded arms.

"You thought he would understand that you needed help even though you weren't able to tell him."

"Yeah, well — " She shut her mouth firmly. No way was he going to trick her into more talking. No way at all.

"What do you think's going to happen if you relax, let down a little?"

She moved her arms lower, tightening them.

"Every time you do it, it gets easier."

"Boy," she said, keeping her voice even. "You're really a profound guy."

There was something disappointed in his expression

and as he picked up his coffee mug, she knew she was safe. For now.

"Beverly," he started.

The phone buzzed, which meant they were running overtime. She jumped up, heading for the door.

He came after her. "Beverly, I hope that next week, we can — "

She left, closing the door hard behind her. Too hard, because everyone in the waiting room looked up. She stayed there, bright red.

"Hi," Maryanne said cheerfully, coming over to meet her, not embarrassed at all.

Beverly followed her out, her hands tight fists in her pockets, watching the floor so she wouldn't have to look up. Once they were in the hall, she walked swiftly, almost leaving her stepmother behind.

"Here." Maryanne handed her the car keys. "Why don't you go ahead and open the car up?"

Beverly nodded, almost running out of the building. By the time her stepmother got into the car, she felt somewhat more composed, arms across her chest, staring out through the windshield.

"You know," Maryanne took her time starting the engine, "most of the people in there have so many problems of their own that they probably wouldn't notice if you walked out with a submachine gun."

Beverly gritted her teeth, the embarrassment back, full-force. "When I want your help, Pollyanna, I'll *ask* for it."

Maryanne looked at her for a minute. "I hope so," she said.

Chapter
Twelve

It was cooler the next day, and Derek was wearing his jeans jacket.

"Everything okay?" he asked as they sat down.

"What do you mean?" she asked, arms already folded.

"I don't know. You seem kind of pissed off. You have a fight with your father or something?"

She scowled. "No." Actually, she had — that morning, on the way to school. She had made the mistake of asking him to please not make her go to Dr. Samuels anymore and ended up getting a long lecture about her attitude. Then, she was late to French and her teacher — Colleen had always been his favorite student — yelled at her. Then, in history, her teacher made a big deal out of praising her research paper and just about everyone in the class scowled at her. In gym, they played volleyball and she got picked last again. Not a red-letter day.

"Something happen at your appointment yesterday?"

"Just drop it," she said.

" 'F you say so." He lit a cigarette without offering her one.

Terrific. She was going to lose the only friend she had. "I'm sorry," she said. "It wasn't such a great day."

He nodded.

"How about you?" she asked.

He shrugged. "Kind of boring." He glanced down at his cigarette. "Hey, yo, sorry," he said, and handed her the pack.

She took one, letting him light it for her.

"Way I figure," he said, "it's okay if you're upset or something, but you should like, tell me so I don't, you know, take it personally."

"I'm sorry."

"Didn't mean for you to apologize. I just — " He fell back on the James Dean grin. "I'm this real sensitive guy, you know?"

"You are," she said seriously.

"Well, don't be telling anyone. I kind of have a rep and stuff."

She laughed. Derek humor was pretty amusing.

They sat, smoking.

"I kind of have a problem with Saturday," he said. "Like, most of the afternoon." He looked over. "And I guess you have trouble getting out on Sundays."

She nodded, feeling a tremendous thump of disappointment at the prospect of not being able to see him for a couple of days.

"You mind?"

She shook her head, afraid that if she said "Yes," she would be too vehement.

"See, it's not like it's any big deal or anything, I just — well, I'm in this baseball league. Just like, a guys' league, nothing big. We have our first game and I kind of ought to be there."

"Where do you play?" she asked.

"The field in the Common. It's really not a big deal, I just — "

"Could I maybe come watch?"

He glanced over. "Thought you didn't like baseball."

"I don't have anything *against* it."

"Well, don't worry," he said. "I mean, I won't feel bad if you don't, you know, want to come." He ducked his head, suddenly very busy with his cigarette, and she smiled.

"You won't, hunh?" she asked.

"Hell, no. 'Course if you *wanted* to, I wouldn't mind or anything." He glanced at her out of the corner of his eye as if, that way, she wouldn't be able to see him doing it. Pretty cute.

"What time should I be there?" she asked.

On Saturday, her father had tickets to the Red Sox game — even asked her if she wanted to come along — and it struck her as funny that they were *both* going to baseball games. That she was going at all, actually. Oliver was going with her father, very excited, in a little warm-up jacket and shiny plastic batting helmet. Maryanne was staying home, making no secret of the fact that she was delighted to have an entire afternoon free to work on her thesis. Since finals started on Monday, Beverly asked her father if it would be okay to spend several hours at the library — until it closed, even. He was in a good mood because of the game and just told her to be sure and be home by five-thirty for dinner. Derek's game was supposed to start at three-thirty, which would give her plenty of time.

She went to the library — since finals really *were* on Monday — and studied until twenty past three. Then, she walked down to the Common, wondering if she was going to have to be introduced to a bunch of teammates, or something otherwise terrifying. Maybe this wasn't such a great idea.

As she crossed Charles Street, she could see the field, and could see Derek at first base, throwing warm-up grounders to the other infielders. She paused, some yards away, to watch. He was wearing a baseball shirt with light blue sleeves, navy blue sweat pants, and ankle-high Nikes. In the winter, he was probably in a basketball league.

He seemed to be a good player, not that she knew much about baseball, but he wasn't dropping the ball or anything, and he could throw pretty hard. He also seemed like he was pretty popular; other teammates shouting things to him, Derek shouting back. He had a Molson sitting a few feet behind first base and when he turned to pick it up, he saw her.

"Hey, back in a minute!" he shouted to the other infielders and loped over to the fence.

"Hi," she said.

"Want a beer?"

She did, but her father would be sure to smell it. "No, thanks."

A couple of other players wandered over, grinning "Derek's got a girl friend" grins. Embarrassed by the scrutiny, Beverly turned partway away.

"Don't worry," Derek said. "They get rowdy and stuff, but they're good guys."

115

She nodded, grateful that he understood how she felt without her having to say so. Definitely a perceptive guy. His friends were closer now, making remarks like, "Who'd of figured he'd have good taste?" and "Whaddaya see in *him*?" But they were friendly-sounding insults.

"Yo, Mikey, Roosevelt," Derek said, and jerked his head toward Beverly. "My friend, Beverly."

"They're just friends," Roosevelt said to Mikey, who laughed.

"Combed his hair for 'bout the last hour," Mikey said to Beverly, who almost forgot her shyness enough to laugh.

"You gonna sit on the bench with us?" Roosevelt asked.

Beverly blushed, and shook her head.

"What," Mikey said, his expression extra-hurt, "you don't like us?"

"Beverly's not the bench-sitting type," Derek said, and winked at her.

Now, she smiled, since Derek had almost never seen her when she *wasn't* sitting on a bench.

"You guys ready to play?" someone yelled.

"We better go," Mikey said, and Roosevelt tipped his cap to her before the two boys returned to their positions.

"Me too," Derek said, scuffing his sneaker in the dirt. "If I can, I'll talk to you and stuff when we're up."

She nodded. "Good luck."

"Yeah."

She watched him jog back to first base, his run a little self-conscious. Kind of funny to see a big athletic guy being clumsy.

There were some bleachers, and she sat discreetly at the end of an empty row. There were a few other spectators: two young wives with children, an older man, three boys about twelve years old. Afraid that one of them might make eye contact, she took her calculus book out of her knapsack and pretended to study. Once the game started, she could focus on that.

Mostly, she just watched Derek, but baseball was more interesting than she'd thought. Not violent or anything. Derek was playing really well too, making lots of outs at first, fielding a couple of grounders. He hit a double his first time at bat; then, the second time, he hit a fly ball all the way to the fence, but the left fielder caught it. Coming back to the bench, he shrugged apologetically at her and she shook her head. He continued to the fence, motioning her over.

"Was trying for a home run," he said sheepishly.

She nodded. "Chicks really go for that."

"Yeah."

"It was a good hit."

"It was a good *catch*," he said. He turned, someone else just having made the third out.

"*I* thought it was a good hit," she said.

He grinned wryly and jogged over to get his glove, one of his teammates tossing it to him.

He came up to bat in the last inning, glancing over before stepping into the batter's box. He hit the second pitch deep to center field, the outfielder catching it on one bounce. Derek ran to second and continued to third base, the ball and the third baseman arriving at the same time he did. But the third baseman hung onto the ball, and he was out. They helped each other up, being jolly, but Derek looked like he might be hurt. Beverly clenched her fists involuntarily, watching.

He headed for the bench, his teammates saying things like, "Good try," and "Y'okay?" He nodded, but his walk was a little stiff, and Beverly hurried down to the fence to find out. But someone flied to right and the game was over, everyone shaking hands. Finally, he came out to meet her, his walk still seeming funny.

"Are you all right?" she asked.

"Yeah." He shrugged. "Hell, yeah." Being cool, he put more weight on his leg, and she saw his face tighten.

"You *are* hurt," she said.

"No way."

"Oh." She flexed her muscles. "I can play, Coach. I can play."

"I'm fine."

"You want me to run, Coach?" she asked the fence. "How many miles?"

"You're being a real jerk," he said.

"You're being *more* of a jerk. Sit down and let me look at it."

"What do you know about it?"

She sighed impatiently. "Enough to know you're being a macho jerk. Sit down already."

He saluted sarcastically and limped over to the bleachers.

"Oh, now you're limping," she said. "What a jerk."

He shrugged.

"Total jerk." She moved the leg of his sweat pants up, careful not to hurt him, holding the elastic wide apart. The left side of his knee seemed to be swollen and she touched it lightly. "I'm sorry, tell me if I hurt you."

He didn't say anything, so she explored the knee

118

with both hands, deciding that it *was* swollen, but it probably wasn't serious.

"I don't know. It might be sprained. Or — " She saw that he was staring at her. "What?"

"Dunno." He reached out, his hand grazing her hair. "Didn't figure on you being gentle."

She flushed, moving away, folding her arms across her chest. "Um, anyway," she said unsteadily, "if you put ice on it, it should — "

"Beverly — "

"Hey, Derek!" Roosevelt came over with Mikey, both of them grinning. "She fix you up?"

Beverly turned her back, bright red.

"Did she kiss it and make it better?" Mikey wanted to know.

"Come on, shut up," Derek said.

Mikey laughed. "Whatsa matter? Thought you — "

"Shut up, okay?"

The boys grinned.

"Later," Roosevelt said.

"Yup," Mikey said.

When they were gone, Derek stood up, adjusting his sweat pant leg.

"You prob'ly have to get home for dinner," he said.

Beverly nodded. Her estimate of the length of a baseball game had been a little off.

"I'll walk you."

"Why don't you take the T," she said, still red. "So you won't hurt yourself."

"I could maybe lean on you," he said, sounding pitiful.

"Yeah, right."

He limped more seriously, walking with great effort.

"It's not *that* bad," she said.

"It is," he said. "It hurts lots."

"But you're going to be a martyr and walk me home."

He nodded sadly.

"Boy, what a man."

"Maybe," he winced, "if I lean on you for a minute."

"What a jerk."

He put his arm around her shoulders and his limp improved. "Ah," he said. "Much better."

She didn't answer, torn between pulling away and moving closer.

"Friends can help injured friends," he said.

She nodded uneasily.

"Look." He moved his arm away. "Maybe I should just walk you."

She nodded.

They walked across Charles Street, not looking at each other, then through the Public Gardens, a couple of workers waving. They walked onto Commonwealth Avenue, Beverly looking at *anything* else. A Coke can someone had dropped. A man in a BC sweat shirt jogging. A boy and a girl walking a bassett hound.

Derek's hand came over, touching hers. "Maybe I'd feel better if I could hold this," he said.

She hesitated, then nodded.

"Nice hand," he said.

"You too."

They didn't speak again until they were in front of her building.

"I-I think I'm late," Beverly said.

"Yeah," he said.

They dropped hands.

"Take care of your knee," she said.

"Yeah."

Feeling very awkward, she backed up the front steps. "Bye."

He nodded, then suddenly came after her in two great jumps, grabbing her around the waist and kissing her. He broke away with a huge grin.

"Derek — "

"See ya!" He jumped down the steps and jogged down the block.

"Wait, I — "

He was already around the corner.

Chapter Thirteen

She stood there, feeling almost dazed, then took out her keys. When she let herself into the apartment, they were eating dinner.

"Where have you been?" her father asked, angry.

"Sorry." She closed the door. "I lost track of time."

"Where have you been?"

"The library." She blinked. "I mean, I told you before."

"Who were you with?" he asked suspiciously.

"No one." She grinned, guessing the reason for his bad mood. "Sox lost, hunh?"

He came over, lifting her chin to frown at her eyes, looking for signs of her being high probably.

"Dad, let go of me!" She jerked away.

"Nick, come on," Maryanne said. "She lost track of time."

"Let me handle it, okay?" he said.

"Beverly, sit down. Your dinner's getting cold."

Maryanne served her plate: chicken, asparagus, salad.

"Who were you with?" her father asked, then paused. "We saw you, so there's no point in lying."

Beverly frowned. They weren't near the front windows, so how could they have? Besides, she could outbluff him any day.

"Well, I don't know what you could have seen, Dad," she said calmly. "I was alone."

He studied her. "Then, why were you late?"

"I don't know," she said. "I was studying and I forgot."

He looked at her, then sighed. "Try not to let it happen again."

"No, sir."

He indicated her chair with his head. "Eat your dinner."

She nodded, sitting down gratefully. "How was the game, Oliver?" she asked, reaching across the table to get the baked potatoes.

"Fun," he said happily.

"With the possible exception of the sixth inning," Maryanne said, and winked at Beverly's father, who looked amused. Sort of.

"Oh, that's too bad," Beverly said. For some reason, the food looked wonderful and she started eating, hungrier than she had felt in months, even taking seconds.

Her stepmother smiled. "Want to go for three?"

"No, thanks, I'm full. It was good though." Beverly finished her milk. "Want me to clean up?"

"You don't have to."

"It's no problem. Really."

Maryanne smiled again. "I'll give you a hand." She glanced at Beverly's father. "I'll put some coffee on."

"And cookies?" Oliver asked.

"*Lots* of cookies," Maryanne promised.

As Beverly loaded the dishwasher, her stepmother put away leftovers, whistling *Peter and the Wolf*.

"Did you get a lot done?" Beverly asked.

Maryanne nodded. "Did you?"

"Some." Beverly caught herself before whistling too. "Do you whistle that a lot?"

"Every chance I get," Maryanne said, and kept whistling. She took down two coffee mugs, putting a teaspoon of sugar in each of them. "What's his name?"

Beverly stiffened. "Who?"

"The boy who walks you home."

"I don't know what you're talking about."

"What's his name?" her stepmother asked.

Beverly sighed. "Derek."

"Where'd you meet him?"

"The Public Gardens. We're just friends."

"I'm not accusing you of anything — I just—"

"So, you really saw me tonight."

Maryanne shook her head. "A few days ago. I was watering the spider plants."

"Oh." Beverly shifted her weight, the dishes forgotten. "And you ran and told Dad and everything."

"No."

"Yeah, sure."

"He just happened to make a lucky guess." Maryanne glanced over. "Why didn't you mention that you'd met someone?"

"Oh, yeah, right," Beverly said. "Like I'd be allowed to see him."

"Why wouldn't you be?"

Beverly gestured toward the living room. "He'll think I'm going to get in trouble."

124

"Are you?"

"Oh, for God's sakes," Beverly said, and closed the dishwasher.

"Your father and I worry, that's all."

"Why would *you* worry?"

"Oh, I don't know," Maryanne said. "No reason."

Beverly thought about that. "You must not have been very happy when I moved in here."

"It wasn't a very happy time," her stepmother said.

"I mean, with Oliver and Dad and all. I screwed everything up."

"No, you didn't."

"Right." She saw the kettle boiling. "The water's ready."

"Beverly, I really wish you didn't feel that way."

"You're not going to do the coffee?" Beverly crossed to the stove, turning off the gas.

"Beverly."

"He'll get mad if he doesn't get coffee."

"He'll recover."

Beverly shrugged, returning to the sink.

"Beverly, your father and I — "

"How's the coffee coming?" Beverly's father asked, coming in.

Maryanne picked up the kettle, pouring the water into the coffeemaker. "Coming along nicely."

"Wonderful." He rested his hand on Maryanne's back, and Beverly bent over the pan she was scrubbing. She really hated it when they did that. Unexpectedly, her father's hand came onto her shoulder, and she jumped.

"I'm sorry I yelled at you," he said.

She shrugged. "It doesn't matter."

"Yes, it does. I'm sorry."

She stared down at the pan, then let out her breath. "I *was* with someone."

His hand tensed. "Oh?"

"A friend of mine. His name's Derek."

"I see." His hand left her shoulder. "From school?"

"No. He works in the Public Gardens — " She stopped. Jesus, what a way to start explaining. "Well, we just got to talking one day, and — I haven't been doing anything bad."

"Other than lying about going to the library."

"I *have* been going to the library," she said. "I have finals."

"Then when is it that you see this boy?" he asked, his voice very stiff.

"On his break. And he walks me home sometimes."

Her father didn't say anything.

"I bet I'm grounded now, right?"

"Well, I wouldn't describe this as the sort of behavior that's going to make me trust you," he said.

"Fine." Beverly started for the door. "So I'm grounded."

"Why don't you hear him out," Maryanne said.

"I already know what he's going to say."

"How do you know if you don't listen?"

Beverly sighed, but stopped by the door, waiting for one of her father's Pronouncements.

"Why don't you sit down," Maryanne said, "instead of looking as if you're about to run out."

Beverly scowled. "I don't want to."

"Beverly, sit down," her father said.

She sat down.

"Thank you." He sipped some coffee. "Now then. Is there something particularly objectionable about this boy?"

126

She shook her head.

"Then, why have you had to go behind my back?" He glanced at Maryanne. "Our backs."

Beverly reached for the salt shaker, twirling it once.

"Why?" he asked.

"Well, it's not like I'm *allowed* to have friends, right?"

He glanced at her stepmother before answering. "I think you *need* friends, Beverly. It's simply a question of your having the right sort of friends."

Beverly sighed, looking down at the wood grain of the table. No way was Derek going to be the right sort for her father. "What do you mean, the right sort?"

"I mean someone who — Beverly, you know what I mean." He blinked and took off his glasses. Professor Johnson, at a loss for words.

"Why don't you invite him over?" Maryanne suggested. "Your father can meet him, and we can go from there."

Beverly frowned. "Just — invite him over?"

"Sure," Maryanne said, shrugging. "For dinner."

Beverly frowned more. "You invite *fiancés* for dinner."

Her stepmother's smile was maybe just a tad exasperated. "Then, invite him over for *after* dinner," she said. "Coffee, dessert, that sort of thing."

Beverly looked at her father, who was nodding. "When?"

"Whenever you want," Maryanne said, and her father nodded.

"Well." Beverly stood up. "Is it all right if I go see him at work on Monday? To ask him, I mean?"

"It's all right," her father said.

"Thank you." She turned to leave.

"Beverly," he said.

127

She paused.

"Things are much less complicated when you sit down and discuss them. Remember that, okay?"

She nodded. You too, Dad.

After school on Monday, she went down to the Public Gardens. She couldn't find him at first, then located him pedaling one of the swan boats around the pond. She walked down to the little green dock to wait for him to pedal in.

"Hope you learned a lot about nature and stuff," he said to his passengers, the two women with little children laughing, the three nuns smiling. Derek tipped his Red Sox cap to the nuns and they smiled, one of them taking his picture. A little boy was having trouble climbing off the boat and he lifted him onto the dock.

"Hi," Beverly said.

"Hey, yo." He grinned, pushing up his sweat shirt sleeves. He indicated the swan boat with one jerk of his head. "Dig my new wheels?"

"Is this a promotion?"

"No, guy called in sick." He watched another group boarding. "Wanna come?"

"On the boat?"

" 'Less you'd rather swim along next to it."

"I'll ride," she said. She knew he was going to put his hand out to help her onto the boat, which was kind of boyfriend/girlfriend stuff, so she jumped on before he got a chance, sitting on the bench closest to the back, where the driver sat.

"You can navigate," he said.

She wasn't much of a one for boats. "Um, these never tip over, do they?"

He just laughed, and as he pedaled the boat out

into the pond, he whistled the song from *Gilligan's Island* so quietly that only she could hear.

"Thank you," she said. "That makes me feel better."

"Yup. Knew it would. Hey, yo," he said in a tour-guide voice as the boat drifted past the little man-made island. "This is where the ducks migrate in the winter. To hibernate and stuff."

Passengers who heard him laughed.

"Hibernate," Beverly said.

He nodded. "You know it. They dig tunnels in the ground and everything."

"The ducks," she said.

"Hell, yes. You must be a city kid."

She liked Derek humor.

"And," he said, "they build like, these webs, to catch littler birds to eat."

Almost all of the passengers were listening now, listening and smiling.

"Then," he said, "they fly to the ocean to spawn their babies."

"Do they die after that?" she asked.

He looked sad. "Ducks have it rough."

"Boy," Beverly said. "You must be a forest ranger or something."

"Yeah. I'm like a chief." He pointed at the tulip beds near Arlington Street. "Know how we grow those flowers?"

She shook her head, amused.

"Well, I'll tell you. You can do it at home too." He turned the boat, heading for the far side of the pond. "We buy bags of potatoes at Stop and Shop. Just ten-pound bags, you know? We wash them up good, then cut 'em in pieces. We put spices on them so the flow-ers'll be different colors, then we bury them in the

129

ground. And in like, five days. . . ." He gestured to the flowers beds.

"Wow," Beverly said.

"You seem like a nice girl," he said. "Not too bright, but nice. So, I'll tell you a secret." He leaned closer, still pedaling. "If you plant Chunky Vegetable soup, it'll grow."

She laughed.

"Hey, I'm not kidding. I know this stuff."

She laughed again, feeling a strangely powerful urge to hug him. She never hugged people. Never had.

"Enjoy the ride?" he asked, when they were back at the dock.

"I learned a lot," she said.

"Just doing my job."

"Hey, Derek," his supervisor called. "Take twenty if you want."

They sat on a bench below willow trees.

"How's your knee?" she asked.

He shrugged. "Good weekend?"

She shrugged.

He took out his cigarettes, lighting two.

"Um, I told my father," she said.

He glanced over.

"He wants you to come over so he can meet you."

"See if he approves and stuff."

"Um, yeah." She took a puff of her cigarette, not looking at him.

"Hunh," Derek said, also smoking. "When?"

"Whenever."

"You have finals and stuff all week?"

She nodded.

"How about Saturday?"

She nodded.

Chapter
Fourteen

It was a pretty bad week. She was so tired after her two finals on Tuesday — physics and French literature — that she didn't even feel up to fighting Dr. Samuels.

"You look pretty tired today," he said.

She nodded, slouched back in the easy chair. "I have finals."

"How are they going?"

She shrugged. "I did lots of studying." She watched him pour a cup of coffee. "Are you, um," she coughed, "mad about last week?"

He shook his head. "It doesn't work that way."

"But — "

He stirred milk and sugar into the mug. "Some people find it harder to talk about things than other people do."

"Am I like, your worst patient?"

He smiled, sitting down. "Everyone's different."

She looked around the office, noticing that he had a little vase of tulips, as well as the usual daisies. "Is this job really depressing?"

"I find it very *interesting*," he said. "And, sometimes, rewarding."

"I don't guess I'm in the rewarding category, am I?" she asked.

He laughed. "Shoot from the hip, Beverly, don't you?"

She folded her arms, not quite sure what that meant.

"It's a compliment," he said.

She shifted uncomfortably in the chair. "I, um, I don't exactly shoot at any of the right times. The *important* ones."

"Maybe not," he said. "But I think you have a pretty solid moral code back there." He picked up his coffee, looking at her over the mug. "What do you mean by 'important ones'?"

She shrugged, not looking back.

"You must have meant something."

She let out a short, hard breath. "Maybe I meant the times it could have helped someone, as opposed to hurting them."

"Such as?"

"Oh, for Christ's sakes," she said.

He didn't say anything, his eyebrows up, waiting for her to go on.

She let out another irritated breath. "All I had to, for Christ's sakes, do was *tell* someone, okay? Like not telling how bad my mother was feeling, and letting — or not telling that he killed Colleen when I *knew* he did. I even *saw* him after, when everyone else was

132

outside, just kind of — " She stopped, the memory too scary to go on.

"Beverly?"

She shook her head, trying to shut the picture out. The school was small, and word had spread fast that Colleen Spencer was outside — had killed herself or something. Knowing what really must have happened, Beverly had, in the confusion of everyone else running outside, gone to the girls' lav and been sick. When she felt strong enough to come out, the hall had been empty — almost. Empty except for Tim, standing all alone by a row of senior lockers, smiling, rocking slightly as if he were humming to himself. Terrified, she had jumped back into the lav, and stayed flattened against the door, waiting for him to come get her, the two of them quite probably the only ones in the building. When she was sure he hadn't seen her, she was sick again. And again.

Aware that Dr. Samuels was watching her, she looked up, laughing shakily.

"What did he do?" Dr. Samuels asked.

"He didn't — I mean — " She closed her eyes, feeling how hard her heart was beating. When she felt calmer, she opened them. "You know like, those *Friday the 13th* movies? We used to go to them and — they don't know anything about what's scary. *Scary* is quiet. It's — " She shuddered, feeling her heart start up again.

Dr. Samuels nodded, not saying anything, and she listened to the tiny little sound the coffee machine was making.

"You know," he said, "maybe — "

"I don't know why I went over there," she said, and saw his eyebrows go up, "I mean, when I found the yearbook, and saw Susan and Colleen — I don't know why I didn't *remember* Susan. I mean like, I started at that junior high right around when she moved, but you'd think I would have — " She shook her head. "And then like, there's this picture of them during Fifties' Day or something — " She reached across the table to get a cigarette, her hand shaking so much that it was hard to get one out of the pack.

"What did you do then?" he asked.

"I don't know." She got the match going after three tries. "I mean, that whole day was so — everything was out of control. Even Tim — " She took a very long pull on the cigarette, slowly releasing the smoke. "I didn't even have to *go* to school. It was the day after he hurt me in the car, and since Maryanne just thought it was my stomach, she wanted me to — " She stopped. "I can't. I really — I have to stop."

"I know it's hard," Dr. Samuels said. "Just try."

She shook her head, inhaling deeply on the cigarette.

"Why didn't you stay home?"

"I *couldn't*," she said, "don't you understand? He would have — I mean, there's Maryanne saying, 'Come on, a day off won't kill you,' when — " She had to stop again. "*She's* the one I should have told," she said more quietly. "My father would have gotten too — but, I mean, I generally don't even tell her what *time* it is, so I couldn't suddenly — " She closed her eyes, pulling in on the cigarette.

"What happened when you saw the yearbook?" he asked.

"I don't know," she said. "I mean, it was a really scary day. First, Tim was kind of following me around, saying stuff like, 'Think about what I said yesterday?'

134

and like, jabbing me in the ribs or something. Then, Patrick Finnegan — I guess Susan didn't tell him *she* was trying to find out about what happened, because he was asking Randy all this stuff about drugs, and Susan was asking stuff too, and — " She rubbed her hand across her forehead, the whole thing — almost — a blur.

"And then you found the yearbook," Dr. Samuels said.

"Well — sort of. I mean, I was on the yearbook staff, and we had a meeting. Only, everyone else went home, and — " She stopped, remembering another commotion in the hall, this time because Patrick had "fallen" down the stairs. She looked up, remembering Dr. Samuels. "It was scary — I mean, for everyone, I think. Baldwin's supposed to be this really nice little prep school and it's like, all hell is breaking loose." She shook her head, lighting another cigarette.

"What did you do?" Dr. Samuels asked.

"Well — " She should stop. It would be a lot easier to — "I don't know. I was just sitting in the yearbook room. I knew Tim and those guys would end up at his house, getting high and all, and I didn't know if I should go home, or go over there like usual so he would know that I wasn't going to tell on him or anything — and I just — there was this yearbook from my old school — you know how you use old ones so you can plan format? — and I was just kind of flipping through it, and there's Susan."

Dr. Samuels nodded.

"She looked kind of different — I mean, she moved to New York and all, and so she didn't really have a Boston — " She shrugged, not sure of the word she meant. Attitude, or something. She thought about

135

seeing the picture, not quite sure if it were her imagination. She looked and she looked, and there were more pictures, and — "I was *really* scared then. I mean, one minute you think she's new, and the next it's like she's a friend of Colleen's and — I don't know. I just kind of sat there looking at it."

She sat there for a long time, so long that a janitor came in and kicked her out because they were getting ready to lock up the building. She walked around outside, in the general direction of Harvard Square and the T — but Tim lived in that part of Cambridge too. If he didn't, she might not have — *might* not have — gone there. His house looked scary in the darkness, with only the hall light on the third floor on, but she went in. Christ.

She let out her breath, wanting to finish up and just get the hell *out* of this office. "I guess I was like, too scared *not* to go to his house, but I really didn't want to get Susan in trouble. I guess I just wanted to tell him so he'd stop, so he'd know that he couldn't — " She sighed. "I sure as hell didn't expect her to *be* there. When I saw her, I was too — I couldn't even think."

"Is that when you told him?" Dr. Samuels asked.

"No. Randy came out to see what was wrong, and I ended up telling *him*." She shrugged, too tired to waste energy hating herself right now. "Same difference, I guess."

Dr. Samuels nodded.

"It was pretty hateful." She looked at what was left of her cigarette, not even having enough energy to finish it. "Please tell me it's time for me to leave."

He checked his watch, then nodded.

"Thank God," she said.

· · ·

She had finals right through the end of the week, and it was a relief not to have to think — about anything other than calculus, English, and twentieth century American history, that is. She didn't want to upset her father, so she didn't go to see Derek for the rest of the week, not wanting to do anything to spoil his coming over Saturday night.

He was right on time, looking very nice in jeans and a freshly ironed white shirt. And he'd gotten a haircut. Beverly felt both pleased and embarrassed by the thought of him going to trouble like that. She was about to introduce him, but he had his hand out.

"Hello, Mr. Johnson," he said, his voice sounding deeper than usual. "I'm Derek Winters."

"Nick Johnson," her father said, sounding as if he approved. Of the handshake, anyway.

Derek nodded at Maryanne. "Mrs. Johnson," he said, and Beverly blinked. She never thought of Maryanne as being "Mrs. Johnson." "Hey, kid," he was saying to Oliver, then winked at her. "Hi."

She nodded shyly, so tense that she wasn't sure she would be able to speak.

"It's good to see you, Derek," Maryanne said, indicating for him to sit down. "We've heard a lot about you."

He looked embarrassed, and Beverly realized that he was nervous too.

"Would you like some coffee?" Maryanne asked.

"Yes, ma'am."

"How do you take it?"

"Um, black, thank you." He sat, somewhat clumsily, in an easy chair, his posture very straight.

Maryanne poured coffee for everyone, except for Oliver, who had milk, and Beverly, who stuck with ginger ale.

"My daughter tells us that you work for the city," Beverly's father said.

"Yes, sir. Grounds and maintenance."

"I see," her father said.

Beverly closed her eyes. This was it.

"My father's in construction," Derek said. "But I just — I don't know. I'm not really interested in that."

"More in — groundskeeping?" her father asked, and Beverly gritted her teeth. Did he have to be such a jerk about it?

But Derek was grinning. "Be something to work in Fenway Park, wouldn't it?"

Her father perked up. "Sox fan?"

"Absolutely, sir."

"Catch many games?"

"As many as I can, sir."

"Well," Beverly's father said, sounding pleased. He picked up his coffee cup and Beverly relaxed a little. Only, now what? She looked at Maryanne for help, but she was cutting cake and passing it around. Oliver was leaning against Derek's knee, smiling shyly, and Beverly was startled to notice that it was exactly the same shy smile she had.

"Hi," Oliver said.

"Hey, kid." Derek ruffled his hair. "How you doing?" Oliver giggled.

"You're what, 'bout ten years old? Eleven maybe?" Oliver giggled harder.

"Hey, how should I know?" Derek lifted him onto his lap. "You're a pretty big guy."

"Sure am," Oliver said, his chest visibly expanding.

"Do you have younger brothers and sisters, Derek?" Maryanne asked.

"No, ma'am," Derek said. "Just wish I did."

Oliver smiled up at him. "You look like Beverly's friend from before."

For a few seconds, it was scarily silent, Beverly able to hear her heart beating.

"Maybe a little," Maryanne said smoothly. "Come here and have some cake."

Oliver climbed off Derek's lap, taking a plate from her. "Don't you think they look the same, Mommy?"

Beverly closed her eyes, afraid to look at her father.

"You do," Oliver was saying to Derek.

"Yeah?" Derek said. "Well, I'm a new friend." He pointed at Jason, asleep and wheezing across the room. "That your dog?"

"Yeah! Want to see his tricks?"

"Oh, absolutely," Derek said and Oliver brought Jason over, noisily demonstrating "Sit," "Shake," and "Lie Down."

During this, Beverly glanced at her stepmother, who gave her an approving nod; then at her father, who was expressionless, but in a benign sort of way.

After that, things went a little better. Her father pumped him some more, wanting to hear about his parents, his brother, his future plans; then Derek asked questions about what he and Maryanne did, Oliver interrupting every so often. Beverly didn't say anything, unless someone asked her a direct question. Mostly, she nodded and sipped her ginger ale.

"Well," Beverly's father said after Maryanne took Oliver in to bed, and it seemed as if the interrogation might be over.

Derek finished his coffee. "Sir, is it all right if I take

139

your daughter out for a" — he grinned — "diet 7-Up?"

Beverly's father studied him before answering. "Bring her back early," he said finally.

"Yes, sir. Absolutely." Derek looked at her. "Okay?"

"Uh, yeah. I'll go get a sweater." She hurried up to her room, almost stunned that she had *permission* to go out. Her father approved. Her father actually approved of him.

It took a few minutes to get out — Derek waiting for Maryanne to come back so he could thank her and everything, and when they finally got outside, Beverly sank onto the front steps, exhausted.

"That wasn't so bad," Derek said.

She laughed weakly.

"Didn't make *too* bad of an impression," he said.

"You made a *good* impression."

"Sure did try hard." He sat next to her. "Um, look," he said. "About your little brother."

She clenched her fists, waiting for the questions. Like, who was the guy, and how come everyone got so upset, and —

"Little kids talk too much," he said. "Don't know any better."

She nodded, fists still tight.

"On the other hand, guys like me," he touched her shoulder briefly, "guys who are old and stuff — they know better."

She let her hands loosen a little.

"So. Let's go."

"Thank you," she said.

He shrugged. "Let's go already."

Chapter
Fifteen

They went to Brigham's where Derek — naturally — ordered a cheeseburger, french fries, chocolate milkshake, and a vanilla one for her.

"You just had two pieces of cake," she said.

"Yeah." He gestured toward the milkshake. "Drink up. Bet your stomach's killing you."

Obediently, she took a sip.

"Feel better?"

She did, actually. "Yeah."

"Well, good," he said, and drank some of his own.

Beverly couldn't think of anything to say, so she kept sipping.

"Your father's an okay guy."

She scowled. "He was being a real jerk to you."

"Cares about you, is all."

Cared about his reputation, more likely.

"Your stepmother's pretty cool."

She shrugged, clenching her fist under the table. *Now* it was question time.

"Want a cigarette?" he asked.

She looked up, surprised and relieved. Not exactly the question she had been expecting.

"What the hell," he said, taking out his Marlboros and lighting two. He put one of them in her mouth, then let his hand rest against her cheek.

Beverly sat very still, not sure if she was going to burst into tears or jerk away from him.

"You have a hell of a time making it through the day, don't you," he said gently.

She hesitated, but nodded.

"I'm sorry," he said. "Wish you didn't."

She shrugged, turning her fork in a slow circle on the table.

"You know, nothing's *that* bad," he said. "I mean, if you're afraid I'll — "

Now she pulled away, still not looking at him.

"Okay. Forget it." He sat back too. "Drink up," he said, indicating her milkshake. "Time you started getting healthy."

"I'm healthy," she said.

"Hate to see you when you're sick then."

She hunched over, not looking at him.

"Makes it worse," he said.

"What?"

"Folding your arms." He demonstrated. "Looks like you think someone's going to hit you."

"I like to be prepared," she said stiffly. Except that she hadn't been. That first punch, smashing into her lip and teeth, had caught her completely off guard. She'd stood there, too dazed to move or speak, and Tim kept swinging until she was on the floor, kept

142

swinging until — she closed her eyes, trying to force the image out of her mind.

"You okay?" Derek asked. "Your ulcer bothering you?"

Nice to have a crutch handy. "Yeah."

"You want I should take you home?"

"I'm fine." She gestured toward the waitress. "Here comes your food."

"Would you like anything else?" the waitress asked, after serving him.

He nodded. "Yeah. Could you bring my friend a dish of strawberry ice cream please?"

Beverly stared at him. "Derek!"

"Please," he said to the waitress.

"Derek, I really don't want any ice cream."

"Didn't want the milkshake either." He picked up his cheeseburger. "Have some french fries."

She laughed, shaking her head.

"Strawberry's kind of cute, know what I mean?" he said when her ice cream came. "All pink and stuff."

"You ordered me *cute* ice cream?"

"Don't seem the maple walnut type."

"More the rocky road type," she said wryly.

"Hey, yo. You getting deep or something?"

She laughed again. "Eat your cheeseburger, Derek."

They didn't say much, but Beverly had a nice time. She ate the whole bowl of ice cream even.

" 'F I ordered you a banana split, bet you'd eat that too," he said.

"If you order me a banana split, you're going to be *wearing* it."

He grinned, running his hand through his hair, which fell neatly into place. "You know me. Feel naked without a hat."

143

That was a cue for her to acknowledge his haircut, but she felt shy and put out her cigarette instead.

"Well." He glanced at the check and put some money on the table. "Guess we should get out of here."

"Um — " She stopped her hand halfway to her pocket. "Shouldn't I — ?"

"Come on," he said. "Told your father I'd have you back early."

It was nice on the street. Quiet. Warm, without being hot. They still didn't talk much, and crossing Newbury Street, he put a protective hand on her back, leaving it there long after they had crossed safely.

"So," he said when they were standing in front of her brownstone.

She nodded.

"Have to work tomorrow. Leastways, until five."

She nodded.

"You feel like — I don't know — doing something? A movie or something?"

She nodded. "I'll tell you all about it after."

He looked startled, then grinned. "Sounds fun."

The street seemed *too* quiet now, and Beverly watched a taxi coast past them.

"Well," he said. "Don't want your father getting mad."

"Yeah."

He leaned toward her, hesitated, and moved back. "Uh, okay if I stop by after work tomorrow?"

She nodded.

"Okay." His grin was shy. "See ya."

"Derek?"

He turned.

"I like your haircut," she said and hurried up the steps without looking back.

After seeing Derek three days in a row — they went to the movies Sunday night, and just hung out Monday night — she felt much more relaxed at Dr. Samuels' office.

"Glad to have your finals over?" he asked.

She nodded.

"How do you think you did?"

She already knew, actually. She had gone by the school the day before to clean out her locker, and the final class rankings had already been posted. "I came in second."

"That's terrific," he said.

"Not really. Dennis Gates should have, but he didn't study for physics."

"And you did."

She managed not to sigh. "Yeah."

"You must be proud of yourself."

"Oh, yeah," she said. "Terribly."

"What did your father say?"

She hadn't even *told* her father. "Nothing much."

"I'm sure he's proud of you."

"Oh, yeah. Took an ad out in *The Crimson*."

"Did you tell him about it?"

She was going to lie, but blushed before she could. "I didn't think so."

"What's the point?" she asked defensively. "He'll make me go to graduation."

"Why, particularly?"

Beverly sighed. "The person who comes in second is supposed to make a goddamn speech."

"That would be tough," Dr. Samuels said.

That was an understatement. "I told the Guidance Office I wasn't going to be there, so they'd tell Dennis."

Dr. Samuels nodded. "I think you should tell your father too. It would make him happy."

"Oh, yeah. Deliriously."

"You know," he said, "she might not have studied either."

Beverly shook her head. "Colleen *always* studied."

"That doesn't guarantee anything."

"She was way ahead. I mean, it was really stupid — I didn't have to do that well."

"That would have been stupid."

Beverly shrugged.

It was quiet for a minute.

"I met someone," she said.

"Oh?" His expression and voice were very interested.

"Yeah." She drummed lightly on the arm of her chair. "He's a really nice guy."

Dr. Samuels nodded.

"I mean, we're just friends and stuff. We're not — well, you know."

"Someone from your school, or — ?"

"He graduated last year. From Boston-English." She checked his expression again. Pleasantly interested, but definitely waiting. Now she was going to have to keep talking. Great. "He, uh, he came over to my house the other night to meet my father and everything."

"How did that go?" Dr. Samuels asked.

"They liked him. I mean, my father let me go out with him after, and Sunday and all."

"What did you do?"

"Well — " She frowned. "Does it matter?"

"Just curious."

"Well, we — " She stopped. "Is it just me, or are they going to put that on your tombstone?"

"They're going to put that on my tombstone," he said, smiling. "What's he like?"

"Tall." She flexed her muscles. "Big." Cute.

Dr. Samuels nodded.

"You probably want more than that."

Dr. Samuels nodded.

"He smokes Marlboros."

Dr. Samuels grinned, and Beverly found herself grinning back.

"Just that kind of guy," he said.

"Yeah." There was such a nice feeling in the room that she was embarrassed, and leaned forward to get a cigarette. She was definitely smoking too much these days. Maybe she'd try to work on just holding them and not inhaling as often. She shook out the match and leaned back in her chair. Dr. Samuels was also leaning back, eating a corn muffin. She hadn't wanted one.

"He's really nice," she said. "I mean, he's about the *nicest* person I've ever met. He's just — I don't know. He looks all big and tough, but he turns out to be really gentle and like little kids and everything. Like, he stops and pats dogs all the time." Picturing Derek playing with a little golden retriever puppy as they'd walked back to her apartment on Sunday keyed off another memory, one bad enough to make her stiffen.

"What?" Dr. Samuels asked.

"I — " Beverly shuddered. "Jesus." She looked up. "We were going to run over a dog once," she said slowly. "I mean — Jesus. I guess I thought he was kidding."

"What happened?"

"Well, I — " Had it been raining? No, just kind of foggy maybe. She had been so drunk that it was hard to remember. There were other people — Randy? — in the backseat and Tim was driving. Fast. She was the kind of drunk that made speed seem both exciting and relaxing. Fun.

"Beverly?" Dr. Samuels asked.

It was hot in the car. The radio blasting, voices laughing and yelling over it, Beverly blurrily aware of Tim's hand on her leg. It felt nice, warm. Like they were separate from everyone else. Older than the others.

"Ten points!" Someone was yelling. "Moving target!"

Tim's hand left her leg, going to the wheel, and everyone was laughing as he aimed for the small animal — it was a poodle or something. She had been drunk enough to accept it, almost drunk enough to be amused. Except — its eyes were yellow-green, and it was trapped, and — everything seemed slow, but it must have been fast.

"Tim," she said quietly. "Tim!"

She was going to grab the wheel and he must have known that, because at the last second, he put on the brakes and swerved, the smell of rubber hot and strong in the air. In the taillights, she could see the dog running away, one of her hands rigid against the dashboard, her arm hurting from the shock of her weight being thrown against it.

The car was silent for a second, but almost as quickly,

everyone was noisy again, with a lot of yelling and laughing.

"You stupid son of a bitch," someone was saying to Tim, not sounding angry at all. "Someday you won't be able to stop in time."

And Tim was laughing. "I *always* stop in time," he said. He looked at Beverly, and again, it was as if they were alone as he reached into the back and got another beer, opening it and drinking some before handing the can to her. "I was just kidding," he said. "They know how to get out of the way."

But it was wrong. She knew it was wrong.

"You pissed off?" he asked.

She was, but she was also tired, drunk, and confused. The dog was long gone, and it seemed easier to gulp the beer, everything pleasantly blurry by the time she was halfway through another, and when he put his arm around her, she leaned against him.

"Beverly?" Dr. Samuels asked, very quiet.

She shook her head, rubbing her eyebrows to try and get rid of her headache. Later, after they'd dropped everyone off, Tim pulled onto a deserted side road and, drunk enough to have pretty much forgotten why she had been angry, she didn't protest. About anything.

She looked up at Dr. Samuels. "Drunk isn't much of an excuse, is it?"

"Probably not," he said.

"I mean, I would just *let* him — " Except that wasn't quite true, either. "I let him do things even when I *wasn't* drunk," she said finally.

He nodded.

149

"Do you think — I mean, is there something *really* wrong with me? Would I have" — she shuddered, even thinking such a thing — "followed Charles Manson around or something?"

"Do *you* think you would have?"

"Well, I — " She thought about Charles Manson's eyes, about how when he was on television, coming up for parole or something; even the reporters seemed mesmerized — by the insanity? The evil? Tim's eyes had changed so gradually that maybe no one else had noticed. Or maybe, after he hit her, she never saw his eyes any other way again. To other people, he looked — cool. Confident. *Normal.* "I don't think I wouldhave," she said, uncertainly.

"For what it's worth," Dr. Samuels said, "I don't think so either."

"He, um, he wasn't always like that. Tim, I mean. I think he only *really* cracked up those last couple of days." The way he looked at her in the car, watching her crumpled over in pain from having been punched in the stomach, saying softly, "I wish you cried, Bev. I like it a whole lot better when girls cry." And his eyes had that blank vicious pleasure in them, the same expression he had had when she had seen him in the hall, humming to himself after killing Colleen Spencer.

She glanced at Dr. Samuels, wondering if her face looked as scared as she felt. "He really seemed normal. I mean, everyone had *crushes* on him. Really pretty girls had crushes on him."

He nodded.

"*Really* pretty," she said. "Like, I couldn't figure out what he saw in me." She stopped. "He didn't think I was *like* him, did he?"

"What do *you* think?"

"I don't know," she said. "I mean, sometimes — like right after — " She flushed. Her sex life was nobody else's goddamn business. "Sometimes, he'd look at me funny and — it was almost like he was *scared*. Or that he maybe really *cared* about me, or something. Like he wanted to trust me, or — " Thinking about those parts was almost worse than thinking about the scary parts. "I guess I mean he wasn't always a monster."

Dr. Samuels nodded.

"Do you think — "

Dr. Samuels' phone rang, signaling that they had run overtime.

"Do I think what?" he asked.

She shook her head, feeling almost dizzy. Like this was reentry or something.

"Are you sure?"

She nodded, getting up to leave.

"Have a good week," he said.

She paused for a second, looking at the doorknob, and the safety of the hall. "Um, you too."

Chapter
Sixteen

"Everything okay?" Maryanne asked on the way out to the car.

Beverly started. "What? I mean, why?"

"You seem quiet, that's all."

"Yeah. Usually I'm not," Beverly said.

Maryanne grinned. "It's a different sort of quiet." She unlocked the passenger's side, then walked around the front of the car. "Do you want to stop somewhere for a Coke?" she asked, once they were both inside.

Beverly glanced over, surprised. "Just us?"

"Unless we run into people we know on the way."

"Oh." Beverly frowned. "Why?"

"I'm thirsty. I thought you might be too."

"Oh. But, what about Oliver?"

"Your father's coming home early today."

"Oh." Had she and Maryanne ever gone anyplace

alone together? Voluntarily? She'd been forced to do some things, but —

"Or," Maryanne said, "we could head straight home."

"No, I — " Beverly stopped. She hadn't just sounded *eager*, had she? "I mean — well, if you're thirsty."

"Okay then," Maryanne said, and Beverly couldn't tell if she was amused, or just smiling in general.

They stopped at a little restaurant in Watertown, both rustic and quaint. They sat at a small picnic table, covered with a red checkered tablecloth.

Beverly looked around at the sawdusty floor, macrame plant holders, and waitresses in peasant blouses. "I suppose they have folksingers here at night," she said, keeping her expression blank.

"They used to," her stepmother said, looking at the menu.

"Did you hang out here?"

"Sometimes."

Beverly left the "Figures" unsaid.

"It's not your father's sort of thing."

Beverly had to grin.

"Are you ready to order?" a waitress asked. Peasant blouse, prairie skirt and scuffed leather sandals.

"Do you drink beer?" Maryanne asked.

Was that a trick? "I have," Beverly said.

"Do you want one?"

"Sure," she said evenly. This *was* a trick — relate to the screwed-up stepkid on her own level.

They ended up with two draft Beck's Darks. Maryanne's recommendation. Sort of strong, but okay.

"Your father thought it might be a nice idea for all of us to go out to dinner Thursday night."

Graduation. Beverly sipped some Beck's. It tasted

better when you got used to it. "My father didn't mention it."

"I guess he didn't get a chance."

"Oh," Beverly said. "That must be it."

"Do you want to invite Derek?"

"*Fiancés* come to dinner."

"Right." Maryanne picked up her beer. "Well, if you change your mind — "

Beverly shook her head, wishing she had a cigarette. But, no point in mentioning that.

"Are you and Derek doing anything tonight?"

"Why, am I not allowed?"

Maryanne grinned.

"Yeah, well, I wouldn't be surprised," Beverly said.

"Are the two of you going to do anything?"

"He probably doesn't want to."

"Did you ask him?"

Beverly kicked the table leg, just hard enough for Maryanne not to notice. "No."

Her stepmother didn't say anything.

"What, are you laughing at me?"

"No," Maryanne said. "I was just thinking how nice it is to sit and have a relaxing beer."

Beverly frowned at her. "Is that supposed to be funny?"

"That was the plan."

"Jesus." Beverly shook her head. "I don't know what my father ever saw in you."

"Must have been my looks," Maryanne said.

"Oh, yeah. Definitely."

"Then, it must have been my pleasant companionship," Maryanne said cheerfully.

Beverly let out her breath. "Are you going to get mad at me, or what?"

"No." Maryanne grinned. "I can always take it out on your father later."

Beverly stared at her. "You would *do* that?"

Maryanne just laughed.

"Does that mean yes or no?"

Maryanne laughed again. "Do you want to join my aerobics class?"

Beverly blinked. Nothing like non sequiturs. "Is that another joke?"

"No. I thought it might be fun."

"But — I don't do exercise," Beverly said.

"I know. I think you should."

"Healthy body, healthy mind," Beverly said grimly.

"There's probably some correlation."

Beverly scowled.

"I didn't mean it that way."

Beverly shrugged, picking up her beer.

"Well," Maryanne said. "How about some tennis lessons?"

Beverly laughed. "Jesus."

"Windsurfing? Jujitsu?"

Beverly shook her head, still laughing.

"*Bocce?*"

"Can I just drink my relaxing beer already?" Beverly asked.

When they got home, they found Derek sitting at the kitchen table with Beverly's father, Oliver sitting on the floor playing with a Tonka truck.

"Hi!" Oliver said, scrambling up to hug Maryanne.

"Hey, yo," Derek said, gesturing with his glass. Obviously, it was Beer Day.

"Uh, hi," Beverly said, too surprised to respond to Oliver's enthusiastic hug.

"Derek came by looking for you and I told him to hang around for dinner," her father said.

"Oh." Beverly blinked. This was *too* weird. "I mean, good."

"You mind?" Derek asked, sounding uncomfortable.

"No. I mean — I was surprised." Beverly glanced at her father and Maryanne being tastefully affectionate, her father with his hands on Maryanne's waist as she stood at the stove, lifting pan lids to see what he had made for dinner. She looked at Derek, suddenly so happy that he had come over that she almost wanted to be a little affectionate herself. "I mean, I'm glad. That you're here."

Derek's face relaxed. "Good. Guess it was kind of nervy or something."

"Kind of," she said and really had to fight to keep from giving him a little hug. So instead, she sat in the chair next to his.

"Guess what?" Oliver climbed into her lap. "Derek was showing me tricks 'n stuff!"

"Oh, yeah?"

"Yeah, look!" Oliver put the first knuckle of one thumb against the bottom knuckle of his other thumb, covering the separation with his forefinger to make it look like one thumb. "Look!" He pulled the two knuckles apart as though the thumb had been cut in half.

"Oh, no," Beverly said, with appropriate horror.

Oliver giggled and showed her his unharmed thumb.

"Hey, wow," she said. "How'd you do that?"

He giggled. "It's a secret."

"Handed down for *generations* of men," Derek remarked, drinking his beer.

Beverly laughed.

"You sure it's okay? Me coming over and stuff?"

156

"Yeah. I mean, I'm glad," she said, giving him a big smile. "Really."

"Thought we could maybe go to a movie or something after."

She glanced at her father laughing quietly at something Maryanne had said. "I might not be allowed."

Derek grinned. "Already asked him."

Dinner, to Beverly's surprise, was kind of happy and relaxed. Derek ate a lot, but he talked a lot, too. He and her father seemed to be getting along okay, and Oliver obviously thought that Derek had fallen off a Christmas tree or something. After, it even seemed natural for him to be helping with the dishes and saying things like that he was kind of a fan of Brillo pads. What about Silverstone? Maryanne asked. Me, I'm a cast-iron man, he said.

"Mr. Johnson," Derek said, when the dishes were finished, "is it all right if Beverly and I head out for a while?"

Her father nodded. "Not too late."

Her father *liked* him. A friend *she* had chosen. Unreal. She started up to her room to get a sweater.

"Hey, don't worry about it," Derek said, handing her his jeans jacket. "You get cold, you can wear this."

Beverly flushed, but took the jacket, holding it awkwardly in one hand. "I *will* be home early," she said to her father, who nodded. A benign nod, not a stern one.

"So," Derek said when they got outside. "You feel like going to a movie or what?"

She shrugged, noticing that it *was* kind of cold, but too shy to put the jacket on. "Whatever."

"How about we go over to the Sack Cheri and just

see whatever's playing when we get there?"

She nodded.

"You look cold," he said as they walked towards Boylston Street, and draped the jacket over her shoulders.

"No, I'm — "

"Wear it," he said. " 'F you catch cold or something, your father'll be mad at me."

She slipped it on, noticing right away how nice it smelled, rolling the sleeves up to her wrists. Cigarettes, sawdust, grass cuttings. A little motor oil, maybe. *Man* smells.

"Look better in it than I do," he remarked, reaching into the front pocket of the jacket to get his cigarettes, lighting one for each of them.

Beverly smiled, and as they walked, automatically let her hands go into the side pockets. There was stuff *in* the pockets, and she lifted each object out an inch or two to look at it. A couple of packs of matches. What was left of a roll of ButterRum LifeSavers. A soft, neatly folded, navy blue bandana. Some change. A Swiss Army knife.

The knife made her nervous, and she ran her thumb along the outside of the closed large blade. "Um, what do you use this for?"

"Weapon mostly," he said. "Corkscrew's pretty damn lethal."

She smiled uneasily.

He took the knife, pulling out various blades and tools. "Comes in pretty handy. Like, I'm always forgetting to buy beer with twist-off caps and stuff."

"You don't just do it with your teeth?"

He shook his head. " 'F I do, I just end up biting off the end of the bottle and then it's hard to drink."

158

Beverly laughed. One thing for sure, he was quick.

"See, like, it has all these screwdrivers and an awl and tweezers — all kinds of excellent stuff."

Beverly nodded.

"And sometimes, I don't know, when work is stupid, I make stuff, you know? There's all these sticks and stuff around, and — I mean, I make stupid stuff — throw it away mostly — but sometimes, I make little — boats and things." He coughed. "Dumb-looking boats. I just — " He stopped. "Getting kind of verbal, hunh?" He closed the knife completely, putting it in his pocket.

"Like, what do you make?"

He shrugged, his shoulders hunching up.

"I'm interested," she said. "What do you make?"

"Stupid stuff. You know."

"Like what?"

He sighed and pulled a long, thin piece of wood out of one of the top pockets of the jacket, handing it to her. She frowned at it: about eight inches long, very smooth, with six sides, and a point at one end, the other end flat.

"I call it," he paused, " 'Ballpoint.' "

Beverly laughed, recognizing the object.

"Was trying to make a cap and all," he said, "but the wood kept splitting."

Beverly turned the wood over in her hands, amused. It *did* look like a Bic pen. "I like it."

"Oh yeah?" He put the wood back in the pocket, Beverly kind of surprised that his fooling around with the jacket while she was wearing it didn't bother her. "Got one at home you'd *really* like then. Call it 'Door Key.' "

Beverly laughed.

159

" 'F you're nice to me, I might make you a tooth-brush or something."

"Never use them," she said.

Now *he* laughed, holding the door of the movie theater for her. They were early for all three of the movies, but after wasting quarters on video games, ended up in the outer space action one. The theater wasn't very crowded and they sat in the middle, near the left. Derek, of course, had gotten popcorn and candy. Lots of candy.

"Want you eating some too," he said, opening the box of Jujy-fruits.

She leaned over, examined the array of candy, then leaned back, shaking her head. "I only like Raisin-ettes."

He started to stand up. "Hey, no problem, I can just — "

"Joke," she said.

He stopped halfway. "I knew that."

She nodded.

"I did."

She nodded.

"Just, you know, didn't want to burst your bubble." He looked at the candy, then slapped the box of Milk Duds into her hand. "Eat these."

"Chicks really go for that," she said and slapped them into *his* hand.

There were some previews — pretty dumb action movies, mostly — then, the lights went down.

"Arm's kind of stiff," Derek muttered.

"What?"

"Just have to stretch it out or something," he said, and slung it across the back of her seat.

Beverly grinned wryly. Cute.

"I mean, don't want to get in your way or anything," he said.

Beverly glanced around, afraid that other people were being bothered. "Just shut up and watch the movie."

"Oh." He settled himself more comfortably. "So, it's okay?"

She gritted her teeth. "Derek."

"Just making sure."

She nodded.

"Good." He was quiet for a few seconds, and she started to relax against his arm. "So, it's okay?" he said.

People turned around, frowning, and Beverly jabbed her elbow into his ribs.

"I want you to be happy," he said, with his little-boy expression.

"Then, shut up."

"Okay," he whispered, the same people turning to frown.

"Jerk," Beverly said.

"Yeah." He sat back, smiling up at the screen, and looking at him, Beverly smiled too, moving very slightly closer before looking up at the movie.

"This is such a nice blouse you're wearing," he whispered. Loudly.

Beverly pressed her teeth together. "Derek, it's a sweat shirt."

The people in front of them got up, moving across the theater.

"It's lovely fabric," he said.

"Derek, if you don't shut up, we're going to get thrown out of here."

"Aw, hell," he said, looking unhappy. "And I'm

161

supposed to be reviewing it for *The Globe*."

She was tempted to smack him, but he was looking at her with such a cute smile that she just shook her head and focused on the movie. It was a dumb movie — mostly asteroids and lasers — and she found herself watching him instead. His eyes and mouth looked all happy — he pretty much always looked happy — and suddenly, unexpectedly, she liked him so much that she leaned up to kiss his cheek.

"Hey, whoa," he said.

He'd turned to look at her, so she kissed his mouth this time.

"You, uh," he shifted the popcorn to his other leg, "you don't like the movie?"

"What," she kissed him again, "you like it?"

"Well — " He cleared his throat. "Kind of. I mean, before. I mean — " He hesitated, not kissing back. "Do — friends — do this?"

"Yes."

His mouth relaxed into a grin. "They do?"

"All the time."

"Well, hell with the movie then." He dropped the popcorn, bringing his left arm over to put it around her. "I'm kind of an animal," he said against her mouth. "Just slap me if I bug you or anything."

She laughed. "Count on it."

Things got intense pretty fast, the arm of the chair between them very definitely in the way — Beverly not sure if she was disappointed or relieved.

"You *are* an animal," she said quietly.

"Yeah, I know." He withdrew his hand. "Been slapped so many times, I lost track."

"That many women?"

"No. Just that many times." He rested his arms on

162

her shoulders. "Guess I forget myself or something. Especially like, with you being so beautiful."

"I'm going to slap you," Beverly said.

"Yeah, I figured." He tried to move to a more comfortable position, the seat arm still in the way. "Can see why people buy those VCR things."

"Yeah." Beverly swallowed, noticing that the other two people near them had moved. She looked back at Derek, regretting having initiated the whole thing. Things would be different now; him pressuring her all the time, wanting —

"If you'd rather," he said, "we could just hold hands or something."

She nodded, relieved.

"And, you know, look at the movie."

She nodded.

"Like to get my money's worth," he said.

"A financial wizard."

"Yup, that's me."

So, they held hands and looked at the movie. Whatever the hell it was.

Chapter
Seventeen

After the movie, they walked quietly toward Marlborough Street.

"Bet you think you opened yourself quite a kettle of fish," he said.

Kettle of fish. How very Derek. "My thoughts exactly," she said, and laughed.

"Just don't want you to be nervous or anything. I mean," he coughed, "you know. Not feel safe or something."

She glanced over, uneasy now.

"Swear to God you're not. I mean, I'm not. I mean — " tentatively, he touched her shoulder " — like — " his smile was particularly nice " — I just like, consider us good friends and stuff."

Beverly looked at him. "How come I have a feeling you're serious?"

"I am," he said. "I really — I want you to trust me."

They were at her building now and she looked at him, then up at the lights coming from her apartment. Trust me, babe, Tim had always said. She backed up a step, remembering.

"Beverly?"

"It's, uh, it's getting sort of late," she said.

He looked at his watch. "Not really."

"I have to go."

"What do you mean?" He frowned. "Am I like, crazy, or were we having fun a minute ago?"

"I just — " She sighed, sitting down on the steps. "I'm sorry."

"Well," he sat next to her, "kind of hurts my feelings when I don't know what's going on."

"I'm sorry."

"Is it your stomach?" he asked. "Or something else?"

She was going to blame it on the ulcer — it was easier — but changed her mind. "No, just me," she said.

"Will you give me a little hug maybe?" he asked. "So I won't, you know, take it personally?" He moved somewhat closer, his cute smile back. "I think it's nice when friends give each other hugs."

She looked at him, not seeing any resemblance to Tim at all — just gentle eyes, a nice smile, and clean rumpled hair. "You sensitive guys are like that," she said.

He nodded. "I need hugs like, *constantly.*"

She found herself reaching out to rumple his hair even more.

"That's nice too," he said.

Shy again, she withdrew, letting her hand caress his shoulder on its way away from his hair.

"Just a little one," he said. "Won't be too scary."

165

She sat very straight as he leaned over, his arms going gently around her back.

"Feel free to, you know, hug back," he said.

Hesitantly, she let her hands touch his shoulders.

"That the best you can do?"

She let her arms go all the way around him.

"Very good," he said.

"Can we stop now?"

He laughed, his arms tightening. "I'm like, so totally sensitive I need *long* hugs."

She tried to hug back, but was so uncomfortable that she kept herself away a couple of inches, her arms stiff.

"Come on," he said gently, "relax."

She nodded, able to feel herself trembling.

"Get the feeling you don't do this much."

"No. Not really."

"D'you hate it?"

She smiled.

" 'Cause if you hate it, I could stop."

"I don't hate it."

"Good." He turned his head and she could feel his breath against her hair. "Guess it'd be kind of nervy to ask if you *liked* it."

"Yeah."

"Yeah what?"

"Yeah, it's nervy; yeah, I like it," she said, and felt her cheeks get very much hotter.

He laughed, kissing the side of her head. "Can I tell you something?"

His voice was so affectionate that she swallowed. "I think I'd rather that you didn't."

He laughed again. "Right."

"Um," she leaned away from him, "I kind of, um — "

"Yeah," he said. "It's getting late."

She nodded, and they stood up.

"Might be I'll have to come by tomorrow," he said.

She smiled shyly, the heat back in her cheeks.

"Well," he said and reached out to touch her face before starting down the steps.

"Derek?"

He turned.

"How do you get home?"

He pointed. "My driver waits over on Commonwealth."

"I mean it."

He shrugged. "Subway'r walk."

"Are you careful?"

He looked so happy that she blushed again.

"Absolutely," he said.

Inside, she closed and locked the apartment door.

"Is that you?" her father asked from the kitchen.

"Yeah." She swallowed nervously, walking over. "I'm sorry, am I late?"

"No." He pushed his glasses up, exams spread out across the table in front of him. "Did you have a nice time?"

"Well — yeah. I mean — the movie was good."

"Good," he said.

"Well — " She edged away. "I guess I'll — "

"Are you hungry?"

She paused uncertainly. "Well — "

"I could make you a grilled cheese sandwich."

"Really?"

"Sure." He stood up. "You didn't eat much dinner."

"N-no, but — aren't you busy?"

He shook his head, opening the refrigerator. "Sit down. Would you like a glass of milk?"

"Um — okay. I mean, thank you."

"Good." He poured her a glassful, which she politely sipped as he got out the frying pan and ingredients.

"Do you have a lot of exams to correct?" she asked.

He shook his head. "Just a few more."

She nodded, watching him melt margarine in the pan. "Dad?"

He inclined his head in her direction, slicing a loaf of whole grain bread Maryanne's friend Yolanda had made.

"D-do you like Derek?"

"It would be hard not to," he said.

"Does that mean yes?"

He nodded, slicing some Swiss cheese.

When the sandwich was cooked, he set it on a plate with a dill pickle, looking pleased with himself. When she'd come down from Manchester to visit him before he met Maryanne, she'd eaten a hell of a lot of grilled cheese sandwiches.

"Thank you," she said. "It looks good."

He smiled, sitting across from her. She felt too self-conscious to eat, but he took an orange from the bowl in the middle of the table and started peeling it, which made it easier.

She took a bite of the sandwich. "It's good."

He smiled again, separating the orange segments.

The silence made her nervous enough to speak again. "I-I came in second."

He glanced up.

"In the class."

"That's very good," he said.

"I didn't mean to. I mean, I

"You studied very hard."

"Yeah, but I didn't mean — " S
most sure that she could feel her hea
Samuels said I shouldn't feel bad about it
no way to be sure — I mean, I should
shook her head. "I'm sorry."

"He's right," her father said. "You should be pleased
with yourself."

"But — are you?"

He barely hesitated. "It shows something very good
about you that you can come up with that sort of
achievement in spite of everything."

Beverly looked down at the table, wishing to hell
that she had never brought it up.

"Yes," he said, sounding awkward. "It makes me
proud of you."

She looked up, unexpectedly close to tears.

"Eat your sandwich," he said, his voice gentle. "It's
going to get cold."

She nodded, obediently picking it up.

Walking into the kitchen the next morning, she
found Maryanne sitting at the table, surrounded by
open books, jotting notes on a series of legal pads
spread in front of her. Funny that there was a big desk
and special light and everything in the den, and Maryanne and her father worked in the kitchen more often
than not.

Beverly opened the refrigerator. "Uh, morning."

"Good morning," Maryanne said, cheerful as ever.
"Did you have a good time last night?"

"Uh, yeah, it was okay." She poured herself a glass

and stood facing the sink to drink it.
are you going to do between now and the
next week?"

Beverly shrugged, restraining a sigh. Her father, as she had expected, had gotten her a job in the political science department, answering phones and doing filing. She could hardly wait.

"Would you like some breakfast?"

"No, thanks." She sipped her juice. "Um, what are you doing?"

Maryanne shrugged. "Nothing special — just some reading until I have to pick up Oliver."

Beverly nodded. He was taking swimming lessons.

"Unless, of course, you have a more interesting idea."

Beverly shook her head, turning to face the sink again. "Could I, um, borrow some money?" she asked, when her juice was finished.

"You could even have it," Maryanne said. "How much do you need?"

"I don't know, I — " Beverly shifted her weight. "Well, I was thinking, you know, about exercise, and I thought — well, maybe I could get some running sneakers."

Maryanne nodded, leaning back to get her wallet from the counter.

"To, you know," Beverly coughed, "run in."

Maryanne nodded.

"Do they cost a lot?"

"Not really. It depends on what kind you get."

"Oh." Beverly shifted again. "D-do you have to be careful? I mean — well, don't you get hurt if you don't get the right kind?"

"I guess so," Maryanne said, her voice athletically uncertain.

170

"Do they know at the store?"

Maryanne nodded, handing her fifty dollars.

"Thank you." Beverly looked at the money, then at her stepmother. "Do you think — " She stopped uncomfortably.

"What?"

"Nothing." Beverly folded the bills neatly in half and put them in her right jeans pocket. "I mean — nothing."

Maryanne capped her felt-tip pen and pushed away from the table. "Would I be in the way if I tagged along?"

"Oh." Was she that damned transparent? "Aren't you kind of busy?"

Maryanne grinned wryly. "I'm at that stage where I wonder why I ever wanted a stupid PhD after my name in the first place." She turned off the heat under the coffee pot. "Let's go."

"I'll, uh, go get a sweater." Beverly left the kitchen, acutely embarrassed. *Two* outings with Maryanne in *two* days?

It was cold for June, and as they went outside, Beverly buttoned her cardigan, Maryanne swinging an old, heavily-fringed poncho over her head. Her stepmother seemed to know where to go, heading right for Massachusetts Avenue, so Beverly half walked with her, and half followed her.

They ended up in a store that didn't seem to sell anything *other* than athletic shoes. Sort of a scary thought.

Beverly was too embarrassed to ask anyone for help, but her stepmother didn't seem to have that problem because soon, a saleman named Chuck was hovering around, full of advice and questions.

"Do you want the shoe for competition or training?" he asked.

"Well, I don't know," Maryanne said. "I should think that recreational use would do us nicely, wouldn't you, Beverly?"

"Nicely," Beverly said.

Chuck took down various shoes, saying things about cushioned midsoles, nylon uppers, waffle soles, and polyethylene inserts. Embarrassed by her ignorance, Beverly let Maryanne do all of the smiling and nodding. Chuck had her sit down and laced her into several different pairs, mentioning features that helped rear foot control, or prevented chafing.

"Do you have any idea what he's talking about?" Beverly asked when he went off to get another pair.

"None," Maryanne said, smiling away.

Chuck and one of the other salesmen, Gary, decided that one of the Nike models, with a special air-cushioning midsole, was the best shoe for her, and since it was a nice discreet grey color, nothing too flashy, Beverly agreed. Chuck assured her that the color was actually pewter.

"Um, thank you," Beverly said as she and Maryanne walked out of the store.

"They look grey to me," Maryanne said, then grinned. "Want to go find a jazzy warm-up suit somewhere?"

"Oh. Well — " Beverly shook her head. "No. No, I don't think so. I mean — people might notice me."

"Ah," Maryanne said. "Well, how about we go to the Army/Navy store and see what we can find in — pewter?"

"But, won't that cost — "

"Let's be crazy," Maryanne said, and started toward Boylston Street.

172

At the Army/Navy store, Maryanne picked out grey sweat pants, a grey sweat shirt, a navy blue one, some white athletic socks, and a couple of sweatbands.

Afraid that her stepmother was going to pick out even more things, Beverly coughed. "Um, I really don't need — "

"Happy graduation," Maryanne said, carrying everything up to the cash register.

When they were outside again, Beverly holding both bags, paused, seeing a bookstore.

"Maryanne?" she asked.

Her stepmother turned.

"Could I" — Beverly flushed — "go in there and buy a book?"

Maryanne grinned at her. "Throwing caution to the winds today?"

"No. I mean, I know how much all of this — I just don't want to do anything wrong."

Maryanne laughed. "What a pair of athletes *we* are." She opened the door. "Come on."

Chapter
Eighteen

The book was very precise. It was bad to run during the heat of the day, so she waited until almost four o'clock. She felt sort of stupid doing the warm-up exercises, but apparently they were very important, so she locked her bedroom door and did the series of stretches.

"I'll be back in a while," she said in the direction of the kitchen as she left, Maryanne saying something affirmative but unintelligible back, hard at work because Oliver was taking his nap.

The book said to start gradually, so Beverly decided to walk a quarter mile, jog a half mile, then walk another quarter mile. More or less. And, maybe, she would run very fast for the last block or so of the half mile. Yeah.

It was both easier and harder than she thought.

Maybe it really *was* time to quit smoking. Nobody paid any attention to her, which was nice. She did the actual jogging part by the Charles River, since that's what everyone else seemed to be doing. A guy coming from the other direction — he was going fast, so he was probably good — smiled and said, "Great day, hunh?"

"Yeah," she said casually, like she had been running for years and her lungs were working right. He didn't look suspicious, and she ran a little faster, kind of pleased with herself.

When she was back on her own block, walking until her lungs *were* working right, she did the series of cool-down exercises the book had recommended, feeling less self-conscious now that she had actually *been* running. Feeling — legitimate.

Going into the apartment, she was surprised to hear voices. Derek. It must be after five. She was going to run up to the bathroom to take a shower, but they must have heard her come in because he was already in the kitchen doorway.

"Hey, yo," he said cheerfully.

"Yeah." She straightened her braid — the book recommended tying long hair back. "I mean, hi."

"You like being a jock?"

"Um, well — "

"Went out to get you a present to celebrate," he said.

"You did?" She took one step up the stairs. "Well, let me take a shower, and — "

"Oh, see, you don't get it," he said. "Most of being a jock's hanging out afterwards."

She smiled uneasily and followed him into the

kitchen, nodding hello to her stepmother.

"Was the air-cushioning midsole a good choice?" Maryanne asked.

"Oh." Beverly blinked. "Well, I — I mean — "

Derek opened a small paper bag, pulling out a bottle of Gatorade. "For you," he said, handing it to her.

She laughed. "Jesus, Derek." She glanced at Maryanne, regretting having sworn, but her stepmother didn't seem to have noticed. Her father would have.

"Drink up," Derek said.

"Oh, come on," Beverly said. "People don't really — "

"I'm a guy," he said. "I know this stuff."

She smiled, going over to the cupboard to get some glasses. She took down two, then looked at Maryanne. "Um, do you — ?"

"*I* don't," Maryanne said, checking the clock, "but I'm willing to bet I know someone who *will* after I wake him up."

"Yo, you really don't get it," Derek said as Maryanne left the room. "Watch." He opened the bottle, then tilted it up, gulping some. He lowered it. "See?"

"That's disgusting," Beverly said.

"Yeah, but it's what you *do*. It's no good otherwise."

"I'd rather drink it the normal way."

"That *is* the normal way."

She hesitated.

"Please?"

She sighed, but lifted the bottle. She tried to drink some, spilled most of it down the front of her new sweat shirt, then looked up quickly to see if he was laughing.

"Need some practice maybe," he said.

"Yeah." Ordinarily, she would have run to her room

to change, but found herself sitting down, lifting the bottle to try again. This time, she was more successful, and she set the bottle on the table. "Okay?"

He grinned. "Absolutely."

She ripped off a paper towel to wipe off the Gatorade that had gotten on her face.

"Use your sleeve," he said.

"This is only my first day, Derek."

"You're right," he said. "Better give you a couple weeks."

She nodded, crossing to the sink to wash her face.

"Might be you'll want me to teach you how to spit and all," he said.

"Might be," she said through the wet paper towel.

"I know all *kinds* of excellent sports junk."

She smiled, dampening another paper towel. "How was work?"

"Okay." He tilted his chair back. "So," his voice was very casual, "do I get to come to your graduation tonight?"

"It's tomorrow," she said without thinking.

"Oh." He frowned. "*The Globe* must have listed it wrong."

Winsor. He still thought she went to Winsor. Oh, God.

"Guess you kind of forgot to invite me, hunh?"

"No, I — " She swallowed. "*I'm* not even going."

"Could prob'ly dig up a tie," he said, "so I wouldn't embarrass you *too* much."

"Try listening," she said stiffly. "*I'm* not even going."

"Why not?"

She turned away from him, washing her face again.

"Are you really not going?"

She gritted her teeth. "Can we drop it?"

"Yeah," he said, his voice as stiff as hers. "Sure."

She turned around. "What's your problem? I can skip my graduation if I want."

They looked at each other, Derek's jaw as tight as hers felt, then he shrugged.

"You're the boss," he said, and bent over to pat Jason.

Beverly crumpled the paper towels in her hand, wishing that Oliver would hurry up and come down, focusing out the window over the sink. Hearing Derek get up, she tensed her muscles, afraid of how angry he might be.

"Seems like it might be nice for you to talk to me," he said, leaning against the counter. "Seeing as we're supposed to be friends and all."

She didn't say anything, realizing something — maybe for the first time. She already knew that if she *did* tell him everything, he would never speak to her again, but — inevitably — if she *didn't* talk to him, the same thing was going to happen.

"You *ever* going to be straight with me?" he asked.

No. "I hear Oliver," she said.

He nodded shortly, sitting back down. "Guess that answers my question."

She didn't say anything, reaching for a cup to pour Oliver some Gatorade.

Graduation day — except for running, the book said to establish a pattern — she stayed in her room, either thinking, or trying *not* to think, she wasn't sure which. Her father came in at one point, suggesting that she come down for dinner, but she managed to convince him that she *really* wasn't hungry, and he left.

It was dark, but she didn't turn the light on, sitting

at her desk, staring out the window. Not that there was anything to see. The backs of other brownstones. An alley. Parked cars — primarily Subarus, Saabs, and Volvos. One thing Beverly had to like about her father was that he bought American.

Graduation was probably half over by now. The salutatory address would be finished, and maybe now, it was time for the valedictorian. She didn't exactly envy Matthew, having to give his speech, when everyone knew he shouldn't be up there either. Also, Matthew was kind of on the tedious side, and Colleen had always been so — Jesus Christ, she shouldn't be sitting here thinking, she should sleep or something. Not that, with the nightmares, sleep would be much of an escape.

But thinking about one sad thing led to others, and it would be really stupid to — in the light from the window, she looked at her bottom desk drawer, not opening it. She never opened that drawer — hadn't in a year, at least. It was pictures, mostly. Of her mother, of the two of them together. Some with her father in there too. A few notes and old shopping lists her mother had written. Her watch. Actually, Beverly looked in the drawer so rarely — and even then, usually only for a few seconds — that she wasn't quite sure of everything that was in there. Her father had been the one to do most of the packing up at her mother's apartment, and he had collected a lot of things that he thought "Beverly might want someday."

But it would be stupid to open it tonight. Masochistic. Like it wasn't masochistic to think about graduation, and Colleen, and what the hell Tim was doing. Pretending to be a model prisoner, no doubt. Reformed. Which made her think of poor dumb Randy, whose main mistake was having some misguided ideas about loyalty toward his friend Tim. He had helped Tim with Colleen, but Beverly knew that he had thought that Tim was just going to scare her. That the concept of his best friend being psychotic was beyond him. Poor dumb guy. Actually, judging from the way he had followed her when she finally ran to call the police, she probably should have told *him* about Tim hurting her and her being too afraid to do anything about it. Randy just might have taken her side.

Except she really didn't want to think about any of that. She looked down at the drawer. Maybe she should just go ahead and — there was a knock on the door and she flinched.

"Beverly?"

Maryanne.

"Okay if I come in?"

Beverly sighed. Maryanne had a way of making statements sound like such pleasant requests. "It's open."

Maryanne carried in a tray. "I brought you some dinner. You don't have to eat it, but — well, just in case."

Beverly nodded. "Thank you."

Maryanne put the tray on the bedside table, started to turn on the lamp, then lowered her hand. "Derek called, but I told him you weren't feeling well." She hesitated. "Good guess?"

"Such insight," Beverly said.

Something flickered in her stepmother's expression, but she didn't say anything. "He, uh, he said he'd call you tomorrow afternoon," she said finally.

Beverly nodded, looking out at the alley. Her stepmother started to leave, but hung back, and Beverly could tell that she was feeling sorry for her.

"It's kind of dark in here," her stepmother said.

"Yeah." Beverly said. *Two* cracks about her insight would start trouble. "Kind of."

Maryanne nodded.

"Look, if you want to turn on the goddamn light, go ahead."

"It might be more cheerful," she said, and flicked it on.

"Yeah," Beverly said. "Cheerful is exactly how I want to feel."

"Well, I'm sure tomorrow — "

Annie lives. "Don't say it, okay?" Beverly said. "I just — please, don't."

Maryanne moved toward the door. "Well, try to eat something — you'll feel better."

"If you're leaving, can you turn the light off?"

Maryanne paused, her hand on the door, but came back and turned it off. As she was leaving, Beverly found herself speaking again.

"Do you think my mother would be ashamed of me?" she asked. "I mean, if she knew."

"I think she would want to *help*," Maryanne said.

"Do you think she knew how much — " Beverly stopped, not sure if she could say the word "suicide" — "it was going to fuck me up?"

Her stepmother didn't answer right away. "I think she must have been desperate."

"What do you mean?"

"I mean," Maryanne's voice was very careful, "she probably wasn't thinking clearly."

"Oh." Beverly felt her molars clench together. "You're saying she was crazy."

"I'm saying she must have been desperate," Maryanne said, quietly. "And very afraid."

181

Her stepmother's hands were in her pockets, and Beverly was surprised to see the outlines of fists. Maryanne *never* looked nervous. "Whose fault was it?" she asked. "Yours, mine, or my father's?"

"I don't think it was anyone's *fault*," Maryanne said. "Even if — it could have been an accident."

"Yeah." Beverly took a pencil from the mug on her desk, breaking it in half. "Right."

"It could have been — the road was pretty icy."

"And she just *happened* to be up there?"

Maryanne shrugged, her posture acutely uncomfortable. "I don't know." She shifted her weight, the fists more obvious. "It may have just been an impulse, or some sort of tempting fate, or — she may have been feeling so badly about herself that she thought you would be better off in the long run."

"You didn't even know her — how can you say she was that stupid?"

"I know," Maryanne said, her voice so quiet that Beverly almost couldn't hear her. "I'm sorry that I wasn't able to know her."

"She didn't *want* to know you."

Maryanne nodded. "I know." She looked up. "I don't imagine that she heard very nice things about me."

"No." Beverly had enough grace not to be able to look her in the eye. "Not very."

"If it makes you feel any better," Maryanne said, "I *do* blame myself. At the very least, for being a catalyst."

Beverly pressed her teeth together, not saying anything.

It was quiet for a while, then Maryanne let out her breath.

182

"If you had asked me ten years ago what sort of man I would end up marrying, I assure you, your father would have been my last answer."

"Then, how come — ?" Beverly wasn't sure how to finish the question.

"We were just friends. I met him at a party in Cambridge, and — " Maryanne shrugged. "I don't know. We used to run into each other periodically. He was very lonely, and I was going through an unhappy time, and — well, I don't think either of us expected it to end up the way it has, but *I'm* certainly very happy about it."

Beverly moved her jaw. "You *have* unhappy times?"

"Everyone has unhappy times, Beverly." Her stepmother took her hands out of her pockets, but then put them back in. "You know, you wouldn't have liked me any better if I had been ten or twelve years older."

"It would have been less insulting to my mother."

Maryanne nodded. "I wish she had known that it wasn't really like that."

Beverly didn't say anything.

"We weren't even comfortable about being *friends* with each other, but — well, people become fixtures in your life much more quickly than you'd expect."

Derek. She sighed. "Yeah. They do."

Chapter
Nineteen

She didn't sleep well that night. But it wasn't nightmares, so much as just plain not being able to sleep. And instead of worrying about the past, she found herself — at four-thirty in the morning, the first birds starting up outside — worrying about the future. Worrying about Derek. About how she was going to keep him from finding out everything, and what she would do if he did. What she would *have* to do.

She didn't think she was going to be able to get out of bed, but it was raining and she knew Maryanne wanted to get some work done, so she spent most of the day playing with Oliver. She *did* manage to get outside for her run, but it seemed a lot harder and a lot less fun than it had before.

A little after six, the phone rang.

"Beverly?" Maryanne called up the stairs. "It's Derek."

"I'll get it up here," she said. Christ, when was the

184

last time she had actually talked on the phone with someone?

"Can I move for both of us while you're gone?" Oliver asked, the CandyLand board set up on his closed toy chest.

"Uh, yeah," Beverly said. "Sure." She picked up the phone in the hall. "Um, hello?"

"Hi," Derek said, sounding happy, but a little tentative. "You feeling better today?"

"Yeah, I guess." Very tired, she leaned against the wall, his voice bringing her back to four-thirty in the morning, lying in bed, staring at the dark ceiling. "I, uh, I didn't know you had my phone number."

"Well, like, I know where you live, and your father's name — are you not glad I called or something?"

"No. I just wondered."

"Oh." He cleared his throat. "Can you maybe like, go to a movie tonight?"

"No. They're going out, and I said I'd stay with Oliver."

"Oh," he said. "Well, I'd kind of rather watch the game, anyway."

"Good," she said, getting ready to hang up. "Maybe we can do something over the weekend, or — "

"Hey, yo, you don't get it at all," he said. "I *meant* like, can I come over and like, baby-sit with you and watch the game?"

"Well — I don't know. I don't think I'm allowed."

"Well, you could *ask*," he said. "Unless you don't want to see me or something."

Oh, Christ. The *one* thing she didn't want to do was hurt his feelings. "I didn't mean that, I just — "

"So, ask him," he said.

Beverly put down the phone, going to the bottom

of the stairs, her father in the living room reading the paper.

"Uh, Dad?"

"Dinner in twenty minutes," he said.

"Okay." She glanced in the direction of the kitchen. Maybe she ought to run this one by Maryanne instead. "Is it, um, all right if Derek comes over to watch the game tonight?"

He lowered the paper, and his glasses. "Excited about the game, are you?"

"No. But he is." She sighed. "It's okay if you don't want him to, I — "

"I don't mind," her father said. "As long as Oliver doesn't feel left out."

"*I'm* probably going to be the one who feels left out."

Her father smiled, and lifted the paper.

"Is he allowed to have a beer if he wants one?"

"In moderation."

She nodded, going back upstairs to the phone. "Um, what time is the game?"

"Eight-thirty," he said. "Milwaukee."

She nodded. "Okay. See you then."

Derek was early, and Beverly gave Oliver permission to stay up for *one* game of CandyLand with him. She, personally, was sick of CandyLand. There were still a few pans left over from dinner and she went into the kitchen to wash them, Derek and Oliver sprawling on the living room floor to play. They sounded nice and happy, one voice deep, the other one almost squeaky. And there was something jarring about standing in a kitchen, washing dinner dishes, and listening to that. Like that was the way *marriage* might be.

186

When she was finished, she stood in the kitchen doorway, watching them. Derek was propped up on his side, with Oliver leaning against him, both of them intent on the board.

"I'm going to win," Oliver was saying, giggling.

"Oh, yeah?" Derek picked up his Saint Pauli Girl and drank some, his other arm around Oliver's little shoulders. "I'm going to cut you off in that like, Lollypop Forest."

Oliver giggled and shook his head.

"You just wait. Once I start down that Gumdrop Lane — you're history, pal."

Oliver giggled, and made what seemed to be a very good move.

"That's right, sport. Get cocky." Derek noticed her standing there and grinned. "Competition's getting ugly here. 'F you have a weak stomach, might be you'll want to wait in another room."

"My stomach? Weak?" she said, and sat down to watch.

"I'm winning, Beverly! I'm winning!" Oliver said.

She nodded. "Looks that way. Watch out for him though — he's sneaky."

"I am *wily*," Derek said, making a dramatic move.

"Wile E. Coyote," Oliver said.

Derek nodded. "You know it."

To no one's surprise, Oliver won easily.

Derek shook his hand, looking sad. "Good game, sport."

"Can we play again?" Oliver asked. "All of us?"

"Next time," Derek promised, swinging him up off the floor, making him laugh. "Right now, your sister and I are going to get your little teeth cleaned and stuff you into bed."

"You don't have to — " Beverly started.

"Do it for my cousins all the time," he said, and swung Oliver down, bending to be at his level. "Tell you what. Pretend you're that Roadrunner and see if you can be in your pajamas by the time your sister and I get up there."

"Beep, beep," Oliver said obediently, and ran upstairs.

Beverly shook her head. "You should be running a day-care center."

"Three're about my limit." He reached out to brush her hair away from the left side of her face. "You feel okay? You look tired."

Beverly moved away, embarrassed. "I didn't sleep very well last night."

"You still mad about the other day?"

She wasn't the one who was going to be mad. She shook her head.

Upstairs, she supervised Oliver's teeth-brushing, and Derek picked out a Babar book to read to him. By the time Oliver was tucked in, night-light on, door open about six inches to let the light from the hall in too, it was quarter of nine.

"I'm sorry you had to miss the beginning," she said, as he turned on the television in the living room.

Derek shrugged, picking up his beer bottle. " 'Less I missed a triple play, I'll prob'ly get over it." He sat down on the couch. "Sure you don't mind watching this?"

She sat down with a glass of ginger ale. "Baseball's okay."

"You wait," he said. "Time I get finished with you, your like, dream in life'll be to visit Cooperstown."

"The Hall of Fame?" she guessed.

"See?" he said. "You're *already* excited."

The Red Sox were batting — no score, no one out in the second — and Beverly sipped her ginger ale, well aware that he wanted to put his arm around her. But, she shouldn't — at some point, probably sometime soon, this would all have to end, and she should be trying to break away, not getting even —

"Have to stretch my arm out," he said. "Okay?"

She had to smile as his arm dropped casually around her. Smooth.

"You mind?" he asked.

No. As a matter of fact, she liked it. Christ, maybe she should have told him the truth right from the beginning. But he was so damned forthright and nice that he never would have wanted to be around her or — she would have missed out on — Maryanne was right about people becoming fixtures. How the hell was she ever going to get out of this?

The game was pretty boring — the Red Sox up by four runs by the top of the fifth inning — and it was a struggle not to let her head rest on his chest.

"Sleepy?" he asked, touching her hair.

"No, I — " She sat up with some difficulty. "I'm sorry, I didn't mean to — "

"So, take a little rest," he said, tightening his arm around her. "I don't mind."

"I can't, I — "

"Why not?" he asked, moving her a little closer.

"Well, I mean — it's rude."

He smiled. "I'll try to get over it." He smoothed her hair with his hand. "Take a little rest."

She blushed, but let her head sink onto his chest. It felt warm. Solid. "I promise I won't fall asleep or anything."

"You worry too much," he said. "Anyone ever told you that?"

Only half the Free World. She felt uncomfortable being so close to a person, but his chest was so warm and safe that she kind of wished — except that she shouldn't — maybe if she just closed her eyes for a *minute*.

When she opened them, the living room was very quiet, the volume on the television much lower. Very embarrassed, she tried to sit up, but he kept his arm around her.

"Um, was I asleep long?" she asked.

"Eight, maybe ten hours."

She twisted to look at him, alarmed. "You mean, they came home, and I was — "

He laughed. "Okay, maybe an hour."

"An *hour*?"

"So what? You were tired." He kissed her hair. "If you want, you should sleep more."

"No, I really — "

"I like it." He grinned. "Makes me feel — manly."

She relaxed a little. "Manly, yes; but I like it too."

"Me, I'm an Ivory boy."

"Gosh," she said. "I never would have guessed."

He grinned, pushing the Off button on the remote control box.

"What happened with the game?"

"Sox won, six-three." He yawned. "You didn't miss much."

"You look pretty tired too," she said.

"What, time for *my* nap now?" He adjusted their positions so that his head was on *her* shoulder. "Can I hear a little story maybe?"

"Right."

"Or, you could sing me a song?"

"You're the one with the trained voice," she said.

" 'You are my sunshine, my only — ' "

"Oh, very nice."

"What, you don't like that one?" he said. " '*Take* me out to the — ' "

She laughed, covering his mouth with her hand.

"Hey, look," he said, moving free. "This *is* like, a Requests Only hour, so if there's anything — "

"Are you *always* so nice?" she asked.

"What?" He shook his head. "What do you mean?"

"I don't know. You're just so damned — sweet."

"*Sweet?*"

"Yeah."

He shook his head. "No, see, I'm a guy — guys don't like to be *sweet.*"

"You are though."

He sank down, sighing deeply. "My rep is just like, out the window."

Maybe she should tell him. It was quiet, they were alone — "Do you ever lose your temper?" she asked, the muscles in her throat starting to tighten from nervousness.

He shrugged. "I don't know. Guess I don't like to see people hurt other people."

She sat up straighter. "Like, what do you mean?"

"I don't know. I mean, I especially hate it when people gang up, and — " He frowned. "Am I answering this right?"

"I was just curious." She moved down the couch to get her glass of ginger ale, wrapping her hands around it. "Is there anything you'd find — unforgivable?"

"I don't know." He grinned. "I mean, if someone got *killed*, yeah, I guess — how come it seems like I'm not answering this right?"

"I told you, I was just curious." She stood up. "Do you want another beer?"

"I didn't mean like, an accident. I meant, you know, *murder*, not — " He stopped uneasily, seeing her back to him. "I mean, *real* murder, not self-defense or — "

"I know what you mean," she said, the teeth-grinding ache in her jaw starting. "Do you want something to eat while I'm in there?"

"Wait, I — "

"I'll see what we have," she said, and went into the kitchen.

She avoided him for the next couple of days, telling him she was tired one night, and that she didn't feel good the next. The only thing she *did* do was go running. Which was getting easier. Plus, there was no competition, and no one thought it was strange if you were alone. Her kind of activity.

Finishing her mile — she'd taken another book out of the library, which was equally stern about working gradually — she walked up to Mass. Ave., waiting for her breathing and heartrate to slow down. There was a "Summer Help Wanted" sign in the window of Steve's Ice Cream, and she paused. Significantly more interesting than spending the summer under her father's frowning supervision. Maybe she could just go in and apply, see what happened — but if she did it behind his back, he would be really angry, and — her breathing was back to normal, and she headed toward the apartment.

After showering and changing, she went out to the

living room where her father was finishing up the magazine section.

"Good run?" Maryanne asked from the kitchen, where she and Oliver were baking cookies. Naturally.

"Um, yeah. It was okay."

"Come eat cookies!" Oliver said. "We made *lots*."

"They smell good," Beverly said politely. "I'll come in in a minute." She looked at her father, not sure how to open this conversation.

He picked up Arts and Leisure. "Seeing Derek tonight?"

"Uh — no. No, he's busy." She watched him read, still not sure if she should bring this up.

"Do you want to ask me something?"

She shifted her weight. "Well — they're hiring up at Steve's."

"I was under the impression that you already *had* a job."

"Well, yeah, but — " She sighed. Nice try.

"Is there something particularly objectionable about the political science department?"

She shook her head.

"Well, then." He returned to the paper, saw that she wasn't moving away and looked up, his expression considerably more annoyed. "Beverly, I went to quite a bit of trouble to set this job up for you."

She nodded.

"If you're worried about my watching over you, that isn't my intention."

"I'm worried about the *rest* of them, Dad."

He took off his glasses.

"They all know everything that happened, and they're going to be waiting for me to — " She sighed again. "I don't know."

193

He sighed too. "Why didn't you mention this when I first suggested the idea?"

"I *did*."

"Oh." His eyebrows came together. "Then, perhaps my actions were ill-advised."

His way of speaking amused her suddenly, and she smiled. "Perhaps, Dad."

He started to frown, then smiled back. "If you'd like to apply for a job up there and see what happens, you may."

She stared at him. "Really?"

He already had his glasses back on, reading Vincent Canby. "Sure. Of late, your instincts seem fairly well on target."

"Um, thank you," she said. "I mean — is it okay if I walk up there now?"

He glanced at her over the newspaper. "Perhaps I shouldn't ask if you intend on wearing what you have on."

She looked down. Jeans, green Ralph Lauren shirt. "It's an ice-cream store, Dad, not Chase Manhattan."

"Very well," he said. "Good luck."

The store wasn't very crowded, and a girl came over to wait on her right away.

"Can I help you?" she asked.

"Uh, yeah, I — " Beverly swallowed. "I saw the sign in the window, and — "

"You want to fill out an application?"

Beverly nodded, and the girl took one from below the counter, handing her a pen along with it.

"You can sit down wherever you want," she said.

Beverly nodded and took the application over to a table near the door. She filled it out quickly — since she didn't really have any experience — hesitating only at the part where she was supposed to write down her high school. She was going to lie, but decided that if it were going to be a problem, she might as well find out early on. Finished, she brought it up to the counter and then, too shy to talk to anyone, put it down, turning to leave.

"Wait," the girl said. "The manager'll want to talk to you." She turned to a slightly overweight bearded man near the cash register. "Bill? She's here about a job."

The man came over, his smile both friendly and absentminded. "Hi." He picked up the application. "Let's see what you have here."

As he studied what she had written, she folded her hands, not wanting to forget and put them in her pockets and look unsavory.

"Going to Wesleyan in the fall," he said.

She nodded. "Yes, sir."

"Do you like ice cream?"

"Well — sure," she said, not certain of what the proper answer would be. "I mean — sure."

"But you're not *crazy* about it."

"Well — I mean — "

"Good," he said. "I like to avoid taking on people who like it too much." He patted the stomach. "Profit margin, you know." He put her application back on the counter. "What's your schedule like?"

"I have a-a class" — yeah, right — "on Tuesday afternoons, but other than that — " She shrugged to indicate large amounts of free time.

"Can you come in this Thursday at ten-thirty?"

"What? I mean, sure."

"Good," he said. "You're hired."

Chapter
Twenty

By the time she went to see Dr. Samuels, she still hadn't seen Derek — which was making Maryanne, at least, pretty damn suspicious — and her stomach hurt so much that she hadn't really been able to eat since Sunday dinner. She sat in the easy chair in his office, absolutely *determined* not to talk today.

"Tough week?" he asked.

She shrugged, not looking at him.

"Everything okay?"

She nodded, looking at the sole of her running shoe.

"What are you going to do now that school's out?"

She shrugged.

He didn't say anything, watching her, and she slouched down in the chair, drumming on the wooden arm. Today, instead of making her nervous, the silence made her angry. Angrier.

"I was at Lourdes over the weekend, and I ran into your wife," she said.

That caught him off guard and he laughed, but the thoughtful expression came back. "Are you sure nothing happened this week?"

She nodded, wondering what time it was.

"Well, you seem pretty upset."

"Gosh," she said. "Maybe you should open a Guess the Emotion booth at the carnival." Oh, hell, she hadn't just gone and admitted it, had she? Christ, talk about stupid. She banged the chair arm once with her fist.

"Something about graduation?"

She didn't answer, still angry about slipping.

He looked at her for a minute, holding his coffee mug without drinking any. "How's the Marlboro man?"

Her head snapped up. "None of your business!"

"What happened?"

She turned away, feeling hot tears, digging her teeth into her lip to keep them from starting.

"Can you tell me about it?"

She closed her eyes tightly, pushing her fingernails into her palms for more control. She wasn't going to cry. No way in *hell* was she going to cry in front of him.

"Beverly — "

She jumped up, heading for the door.

"Wait a minute." He came after her. "Beverly — "

"Fuck you," she said and stepped out into the hall, slamming the door behind her.

Everyone in the waiting room looked up, Maryanne glancing at the clock, and Beverly strode through the room, slamming the main door.

Maryanne didn't catch up with her until she was

197

almost at the car. "Everything all right?" she asked, somewhat out of breath.

"Don't even fucking start," Beverly said through her teeth.

Her stepmother started to say something, then looked at her. "Okay," she said through *her* teeth and went ahead to open the car.

"I'm taking the T home," Beverly said.

Her stepmother turned. "You want to take the T, *take* the goddamn T!"

They stood there looking at each other, Beverly breaking the gaze.

"You'll get me in trouble if I do," she said, "right?"

"Grow up, Beverly," Maryanne said and got into the car, slamming her door.

Beverly got into the backseat, slamming that door too. Hard.

They didn't speak all the way home, and once they were in the apartment, Beverly went straight to her room, slamming *that* door and putting AC/DC on her stereo. Loud.

When the knock finally came, she opened the door, preparing to be yelled at.

"It's dinnertime," her father said, and she could tell that he was grinding his teeth too.

"I — " She backed down a little. "My stomach's bothering me." Which wasn't a lie.

"I see," he said. "Well, why don't you come down and sit at the table, anyway."

"My stomach's *really* bothering me."

"I see." He moved his jaw. "What happened this afternoon?"

"Nothing."

He looked at her for a minute, then nodded. "Very

198

well," he said. "Please lower the volume."

Later, there was another knock. This time, it had to be Maryanne. She turned the Dead Kennedys even lower and went over to open it.

"Derek's here!" Oliver said happily, wearing his Mr. T beads.

Christ. Exactly what she didn't want. "Can you tell him — " She stopped. This was Oliver. She couldn't use Oliver.

"Aren't you coming?" he asked.

"Uh, yeah," she said. "I'll be down in a minute." She washed her face, then went downstairs, finding Derek standing in the living room, where the television was on.

"Hi," he said, moving toward the stairs so his voice wouldn't disturb the show.

She nodded, having to fold her arms across her stomach.

"Seeing as you don't talk on the phone, I decided I had to show up," he said.

She didn't say anything, feeling too guilty to look at him.

"Can you come out for a while?" he asked. "I kind of thought it might be nice if we talked or something."

"I — " She glanced at her father, who was sitting on the couch, not nearly as engrossed as Oliver was in the show. "I don't think — "

"You aren't even going to ask?"

She walked over to the couch, her stomach feeling as though it were trying to constrict completely. "Is it all right if we go out?" she asked her father quietly. "I won't be gone long."

He studied her before answering. "Make certain of that," he said.

She nodded, checking her pocket to make sure she had her keys, not looking at him *or* Maryanne.

"You'll need a sweater," Derek said, at the door.

She nodded, walking slowly upstairs to get one.

"Brigham's okay?" he asked when they were outside.

She nodded, so nervous that it was turning into fear.

He took out his cigarettes. "Want one?"

She shook her head, hunched over her arms.

They didn't really speak walking down Exeter Street, and once they were inside the restaurant, sat in a small booth on the side.

"You want a milkshake?" he asked when the waitress had come over.

"I'd rather have a ginger ale," she said.

He nodded. "Could you bring us a ginger ale and a cup of coffee, please?"

"You're, uh, you're not getting food?" she asked, when the waitress was gone.

"Don't have much appetite, somehow." He lit another cigarette, stubbing out the old one in the ash tray.

They sat there for a while without speaking, even after the waitress brought their drinks.

"So, what's the deal?" he asked finally. "I mean, if I said something wrong the other night, I'm sorry, but — I mean, if you don't *tell* me anything, how'm I supposed to know?"

She shrugged, her stomach so jumpy that she couldn't even *attempt* the ginger ale.

"Look, I know you've got this whole privacy deal going, but — it's really getting in the way, you know?"

She didn't say anything, her stomach even more unsteady.

He frowned, lighting another in a series of cigarettes. "Is it something about your mother?" he asked suddenly.

She looked up. "What *about* my mother?"

"I don't know. I mean, she isn't around, you never talk about her — I figure *something* bad must have happened."

She swallowed, gripping the edge of the table with one hand to steady herself.

"I mean, Christ," he said. "If that's — "

"Look," she said quietly, not looking at him. "I don't want to hurt your feelings, but I can't see you anymore."

"Yeah." He nodded. "Figures."

"It's nothing — I just can't, okay?" The tears that had threatened in Samuels' office were back, full force, and she got up. "I can't."

"So, what does that mean? You just — "

She shook her head, the tears so close now that she had to leave, hurrying for the door.

"Beverly, wait — Christ." He took out a couple of dollars and dropped them on the table before coming after her.

She turned down Exeter Street, walking as swiftly as she could, her stomach hurting too much for her to run.

"Will you wait for me, for Christ's sakes?" he asked.

"Please leave me alone," she said, not turning.

"Oh, yeah. Let you walk around the middle of the city at night."

She walked more quickly, Derek breaking into a trot to keep up.

"Hey, come on," he said as she crossed Commonwealth. "Come on, Bev, don't."

Tim always called her Bev. She ran now, Marlborough Street only a block away.

He caught up to her in front of her brownstone, taking her arm. "Come on," he said. "Can't we at least — "

She jerked free, scared now. "Don't touch me!"

"I just — "

"Don't hurt me!"

"Beverly — "

"Look," she said, hearing her voice shake. "I don't want to see you anymore. I don't want you to call me, I don't want you to come over, I don't want you to do anything, got it?"

"Yeah," he said, "but — oh, come on," he said as she walked up the steps. "Can't you at least — "

"There's nothing *to* tell you," she said.

"Look, no way am I leaving until you talk to me."

"Right," she said, opening the front door.

He watched her for a second, then nodded. "Okay," he said. "Okay, fine. It's *your* loss."

"Fine," she said and slammed the door, unlocking her apartment door and hurrying inside. She tried to lock it, hands shaking, but before she could finish, burst into tears.

"Is that you?" her father called from the kitchen.

"Um — " She gulped to try and stop crying. "Yeah."

He came out to the living room, holding his glasses in one hand.

"I'm sorry," she said before he could say anything, aware that she was about to burst into even harder tears. "I — I'm really tired." She ran upstairs and into her room, closing the door gently so he wouldn't come after her.

She changed into her nightgown, struggling to stop

crying, and was just about to turn the light out when there was a knock on the door.

"I-I'm changing," she said.

"Are you all right?" Maryanne asked.

Jesus! Beverly yanked the door open. "I'm crying, okay? You satisfied?"

Her stepmother hesitated. "Did you and he — "

"That's none of your goddamn business," Beverly said and, this time, did slam the door.

Chapter
Twenty-One

She cried for most of the night, her eyes, head, and stomach all hurting pretty equally. She should never have made friends with him in the first place, she should have *known* that this would — she gave up on thinking and just plain cried.

It was finally morning and, as she expected, there was a knock on her door.

"What."

Her father came in, frowning. "Beverly."

She lifted her head slightly, not wanting him to see how red her eyes were.

"Derek is on the front steps."

She scowled. "So tell him to go away."

"Actually — " Her father blinked several times. "Let me clarify. Derek is *asleep* on the front steps."

She looked all the way up. "Like he spent the night?"

Her father nodded, blinking again. "Exactly like that."

She sighed, covering her face with her hands.

"It looks quite uncomfortable," her father said.

"Oh, Christ." She reached for her sweat pants and sweat shirt.

He was sitting on the front steps, hunched into the cast-iron railing, his head at an awkward angle, and seeing him, she sighed again.

"Derek."

He jerked awake, looking confused. Once he figured out where he was, he sat up, winced, and rubbed the back of his neck with one hand.

"Did you really spend the night here?"

He yawned, rubbing his eyes, then stood up with some difficulty. "You don't even bring me a little cup of juice?"

"Oh, for Christ's sakes."

"Just a little one?"

She gritted her teeth. "What kind."

"Orange is nice," he said. " 'Less you have grape."

"We have orange."

He nodded pleasantly.

She stood there, realized that he was waiting for her to go fetch it, and frowned. "You look terrible in the morning."

He rubbed his hand across the beard stubble on his jaw and grinned. "People gen'rally do."

"Mmmm." She frowned and went back inside.

In the kitchen, she took a glass down, banging it on the counter, and crossed grimly to the refrigerator. She could feel her father and Maryanne watching her — Oliver oblivious, coloring in his Bert and Ernie coloring book — and scowled. "He wants juice."

Maryanne started to laugh, but covered it with a cough. "Would he like some toast too?"

"Oh, most likely," Beverly said, grimly. She poured the juice as Maryanne fixed a plate with toast, jam, napkins, and a green Flintstones vitamin.

Seeing the vitamin, Beverly scowled harder. "I'm glad you find this so funny."

"Hard not to," Maryanne said, and handed her the plate.

"Oh, yeah." Beverly scowled, and carried the plate and glass outside, putting them on the steps. "Here's your damn breakfast," she said, and turned to go inside.

"It's really sad to eat alone," he said.

"Yeah, well, if you're smart, you'll eat on the way to work — you're already about an hour late."

He stopped chewing long enough to look at her. "Fuck work," he said, and continued chewing.

"That's mature."

He nodded, drinking some juice.

"The vitamin wasn't my idea."

He grinned. "Must have been your father then, hunh?"

She leaned against the front door, tapping her foot.

"So," he said, very conversational. "Are you going to talk to me now?"

"I don't see what the big deal is," she said stiffly. "I just don't want to see you anymore."

"Well" — he stopped smiling, looking — for the first time since she'd met him — genuinely unhappy — "that'd have to be your decision, but seems like it'd be polite to say why."

"I don't have to be polite."

He pushed the toast away, unfinished. "I don't know. I mean, I guess I thought we were — I don't know."

"Look," she said. "I just don't — for Christ's sakes, I don't have to explain it."

He smiled a little, his eyes still very unhappy. "You do if you don't want me *living* on these steps."

"The cops'll kick you off soon enough."

"Yo, come on." He shook his head. "I mean like, maybe I'm a jerk, but I was thinking we were friends and — I don't know."

She didn't say anything.

"So, what happened with the guy who looks like me?" he asked.

She stiffened. "You don't look like him."

Derek shrugged. "Way I figure, he must have done something pretty bad."

"Maybe I don't want to talk about it."

"But *I* do."

She turned to go inside.

"We're friends, remember?" he said. "Christ, nothing's *that* bad."

She turned around. Whirled, really. "Okay, okay, fine," she said, hearing her voice already starting to shake. "You want to hear about it, I'll tell you about it. *Then*, you can see how damn much you want to be my friend."

He shrugged, patting the step next to him. "So, sit down."

"I don't want to!"

"So, don't sit down."

She sat down, several feet away from him.

"You could sit *near* me," he said. "I mean, you know how totally stiff my arm gets."

She looked at him, much closer to tears than she wanted to be. "This isn't a joke, okay, Derek?"

"Okay," he said, more gently. "Don't worry."

"Yeah." She laughed shakily. "Right."

He stayed on his side of the step, drinking his orange juice, and she took a deep breath, trying to start.

"Don't worry," he said, again.

She closed her eyes and started; telling him everything, defensive and nervously defiant at first; then speaking dully, the story seeming even more unreal on such a bright, sunny morning. She started with her mother's killing herself and ended with her skipping graduation, then sat very still, hands twisted together in her lap, waiting for his reaction.

"I can't believe someone would hit you," he said softly.

She looked up. "What?"

"That son of a bitch," he said, reaching out to touch her face, his other hand clenched.

"But — weren't you listening to me?"

He nodded.

"Don't you hate me?"

He shook his head, his smile so nice and kind that, without meaning to, she burst into tears. He moved over, putting his arm around her, and she tried to stop crying.

"I'm sorry," she said. "I just — I'm really sorry."

He shrugged. "Things happen."

"But, I should have — I mean — "

"So, you made a mistake."

"A *mistake*?" she said. "People are *dead* because of — "

"Because of *him*," Derek said. "Not you. I mean, yeah, you should have told your father, but the guy sounds like such a psychopath, he probably *would* have come after you."

208

She wrapped her arms around herself, cold in the sunshine. "But, I should have — "

"So, you were scared," he said. "What are you going to do, kill yourself?"

She looked up guiltily.

"Jesus," he said. "And what would *that* prove?"

"It would have been easier."

"Easier for *you*," he said. "And totally stupid and selfish. I mean, Christ, if you feel bad because you maybe weren't brave enough, doesn't it make sense to tough it out *now*? I mean, Christ."

"I just — I really hate myself," she said.

He grinned. "Could've fooled me."

She smiled a little, still hunched over her arms.

"I mean, not much you can do about it now, right? Except, like, say, 'I did something stupid and now I know it's maybe not cool to try and be like, alone.' "

She smiled a little more.

"I mean, seems like to *me* you've got plenty of people who'll do whatever to help you feel better. Me, that doctor guy, your father — " He paused. "Maryanne's a pretty cool lady."

She nodded.

"Bet your mother was too, except maybe she didn't know what to do about being totally scared either."

Beverly was almost surprised to feel herself nodding.

"So," he said, and kissed the side of her head.

"What about what you were saying before?" she asked. "About not being able to forgive — "

"Oh, hell, I was just talking," he said. "I mean, I thought you were upset because you'd like, had an abortion or something. I was just trying to — I didn't mean anything by it."

They sat there for a minute.

"I'm really tired," she said.

He laughed. "Yo, me too."

"You should be mad at me. I still don't get — "

"I don't know," he said. "Must be because I love you or something."

She looked over, the tears back in her eyes.

"Just so you know." He stood up, stretching. "How much you want to bet your father's in there all uptight because he isn't at work yet?"

She had to smile. "I bet you're right."

"So." He put his hand out to help her up. "How about we go inside, and you let me use your phone and I can tell my boss I'm sick or whatever."

She nodded, slowly standing up.

"And maybe we can like, make me a little more breakfast?"

She smiled. "Do you like French toast?"

"I *love* French toast," he said.

Chapter
Twenty-Two

Oliver was delighted to have French toast with them. Her father was delighted to be able to leave for work. Knowing Maryanne, she was just plain delighted. Not that Beverly told them anything, but it was probably pretty obvious that there had been some kind of mood change.

"Ah." Derek pushed his plate away, finishing the last of his coffee. "That's more like it."

"You don't want another couple of loaves?" Beverly asked.

"No, this'll hold me till lunch."

"It'll hold *me* until Friday," she said.

Oliver held up his plate. "Can I have more?"

"You're supposed to say, 'May I?' " she said automatically.

"May I?"

She lifted a piece from her own plate. "Take this one — I haven't touched it."

"Boy," Oliver poured little circles of maple syrup on it, "I can eat more'n *Derek* even."

"Sure looks that way." Derek yawned. "I'm starting to lose it here."

"Maybe you should go home and sleep," Beverly said.

He nodded. "I'd, you know, stay and talk to you and all, but" — he shook his head — "might not be as entertaining as usual."

"And you have a rep and stuff," she said.

"Yeah." He carried both of their plates over to the sink, rinsing them.

"Don't worry," Beverly said, "I can — "

"What, are you kidding?" He put the plates and silverware into the dishwasher. "Chicks *totally* go for guys who do housework." He pointed a spatula at Oliver. "Remember that."

Oliver nodded seriously, bringing his plate over.

After the dishes were finished, Beverly walked with him to the front door.

"Prob'ly be a good idea for you to take a little rest too," he said.

She nodded.

"I'll call you when I wake up?"

She nodded.

"Good." He took her hand, giving it a little squeeze. "My day off's Thursday this week — you feel like doing something fun?"

"I, um, I have to work, actually," she said.

"Oh, right. Your father — "

"I got a job at Steve's," she said, kind of pleased by the sound of that. "The one on Mass. Ave."

"Yo, excellent," he said, then grinned. "So. You get a discount?"

She was amazed that she could feel so much better, so quickly. Not that it was a miracle cure or anything, but life in general just seemed easier. Like an albatross had flown off her shoulders or something. She was hungrier at meals, she didn't have as many nightmares, she felt strong enough to run the whole mile, instead of walking half of it. Even the job wasn't as scary as she had anticipated, although scooping rock-hard ice cream seemed, so far, like an excellent way to pull all of the muscles in one's forearm.

Except she *wasn't* looking forward to seeing Dr. Samuels.

"Hi," he said, by the coffee machine when she came in. "How was your week?"

She stayed by the door. "Am I in trouble?"

"What do you think?"

"I'm sorry," she said. "I was really rude."

"I hope everything's better." He indicated the machine. "Do you want anything?"

She shook her head, sitting down. She crossed her legs, then folded her hands. Dr. Samuels carried over a cup of coffee, then held his cigarettes in her direction.

"I'm, um, cutting down," she said. It seemed sort of imbecilic to be running, and trying to be healthy, and then smoke constantly.

"Good for you," he said, and sat down. "So. How's your friend?"

She smiled sheepishly. "Fine."

He lifted his eyebrows.

"I sort of told him everything," she said. "I mean,

instead of waiting to see if he was going to hate me when he found out."

"Which, I gather, he didn't."

"Well — no." She frowned, still surprised by it. "He didn't seem to mind at all."

"That's good, isn't it?"

She nodded. "My father and Oliver went to a baseball game with us."

"Was it fun?"

"*They* sure had fun."

"You didn't?"

"Well, sort of," she said. "I mean, I'm still not so sure about baseball."

Dr. Samuels nodded.

"I mean, Derek was talking about how practically the happiest job he could imagine would be making baseball bats. You know, hand-sanding the wood and all."

Dr. Samuels nodded.

"He says aluminum bats are un-American."

Dr. Samuels laughed. "Did your father agree?"

"Oh, yeah, completely." In fact, the way they went on and on about it, probably even Senator McCarthy would have thought that they were getting carried away with the un-American business.

"I gather your stepmother doesn't like baseball much?" he asked.

"Well, sort of. Lately, she just works on her damn thesis."

He nodded.

"That was a direct quote," she said. "Not me being rude or anything."

He nodded. "How do you feel about her these days?"

214

Reading you loud and clear, Dr. Samuels. "I got a job at Steve's," she said.

"Good for you," he said. "Do you like it?"

"It's okay. I've only had to do it three times."

He nodded his interested nod.

"Maryanne brought Oliver up for some ice cream on Saturday. I thought it was sort of embarrassing, but other people at work said their families show up sometimes too." Families. Christ, a Freudian slip. And from the way he nodded, she could tell that he had noticed too. "Anyway," she said, "the job's not so bad."

It was quiet.

"Okay, so I like her," she said. "Is that such a damn crime?"

He grinned. "No."

"I mean, she's a goddamn *doormat*, but — " Beverly shrugged.

"How is she a doormat?"

"Well, she — how do you *think*?"

"Just in general," he said.

"Well — yeah. I mean, she's so busy being *reasonable*, that you can practically kick her in the teeth and she just stands there smiling, you know?" Beverly shook her head. "If I were her — she — there're a bunch of times I would have smacked me."

"You give her a hard time?"

"Sure. I mean — she even likes coming here, so she can just sit and read for an hour. If it rains, she goes out for a walk in it. You could put her in the goddamn *lion's* den, and she'd say" — Beverly put on a Maryanne happy face — " 'Hey, guys, I know a great place to get steaks in Saugus — feel like going?' " Beverly grinned wryly. "And you want to know the stupid thing?"

He nodded.

"They'd *go*." She shook her head. "They'd have *fun*." She had to grin. "They'd keep in *touch*."

Dr. Samuels laughed. "She sounds like a very positive person."

"A damn doormat," Beverly said, finished with the subject.

"How do she and your father get along?"

Not finished. Okay. "I don't know," she said. "They seem like they're happy."

He nodded.

"It's like — well, this is stupid, but it's like he's a balloon or something, and she walks around letting air out so he'll act normal. Not be so uptight."

He nodded.

"Sometimes — I don't think he and my mother were very good influences on each other. Like, people *should* be more different."

He nodded.

"I don't know." It was quiet again, and she sighed. "I think about my mother lately."

"How so?"

"I don't know. Just in general."

He nodded. "Why do you think you've started thinking about her?"

"I don't know. I just do." She swallowed. "Before, I always used to cry, but now it seems like I can think about it."

"That's good."

"I guess." She let out her breath. "Maryanne said that it wasn't anyone's fault, but that she *feels* like it was hers."

"Do you agree?"

"I don't know. Probably not."

216

"Do you think it was anyone's fault?"

"I don't know." Beverly thought about that, but shook her head. "I really don't know."

"Do you ever think it was your fault?"

"No," she said. "I mean, yeah, but I know that's stupid."

He nodded.

"I mean, Maryanne said — " She stopped. What was she doing quoting Maryanne all over the place?

"What did Maryanne say?"

She sighed. "You're starting to annoy me."

"Just curious."

Right. She sighed again. "She said that she must have been really scared and desperate, and that it *might* have been an accident. Like, it was subconscious, I guess, but maybe she didn't really mean for it to happen."

He nodded.

"It could be true," she said, and felt her jaw tighten. "I, personally, think she just went and ran her car the hell off the road."

He nodded.

"But, I don't know. I mean, if she were going to do it on purpose, you'd think she would have waited until I was somewhere with my father, instead of doing it with me sitting at home in front of the stupid Christmas tree, wondering where the hell she was."

He nodded.

"It's hard not to take it personally," she said.

"I can see why it would be hard, but I doubt that she meant it that way."

"I think Maryanne thinks she killed herself too, but was too nice to say so."

"Could be," he said.

"But, I'll never really know, right? And there's not much I can do about it at this point, anyway."

"Forgive her, maybe," he said.

She smiled a little. "Maybe."

The phone buzzed and she glanced over at it, startled. "It's over already?"

He nodded, his eyes amused.

"I mean, Christ," she said, flushing. "It's about time."

He laughed. "Have a good week."

"I still maybe think you're a jerk."

He laughed again.

"Well." She stood up. "See you next week."

Chapter
Twenty-Three

Her shift was almost over on Thursday afternoon when Derek showed up.

"Hello, miss," he said, taking off his baseball cap. "Would you make a milkshake for a poor, tired city worker?"

"No one gets milkshakes here, Derek. You get *mix-ins*." Which was ice cream with crushed Heath bars or raisins or M&M's or whatever mashed in.

"Oh." He looked sad. "But I like milkshakes."

"What kind do you want?"

"What do you recommend, miss?"

"Cinnamon-raisin."

He winced. "What, are you trying to make me sick?"

She started scooping. "Is that a yes?"

"Just make me the most normal chocolate you have."

"Is carob okay?"

He shrugged. "Nothing personal," he said as she

scooped, "but this place is sort of upscale for me."

"Brigham's more to your taste?"

He nodded, watching her make the shake.

"Thank you, miss," he said when she gave it to him, along with his change. "What time do you get off?"

"Six."

"Could I maybe walk you home?"

"If you sit down and drink your milkshake and shut up."

He grinned, heading for an empty table.

"We working the same shift Saturday?" a boy asked her as she left.

"Eleven to six?" she said.

He nodded. "See you then."

"Who was that?" Derek asked, when she was out from behind the counter.

"His name's Hank. He works with me," she added unnecessarily.

"Oh." Derek frowned, looking at him. "He has glasses."

"Yeah. So?"

"Where's he go to school?"

"Brown."

"Oh," Derek said, and frowned more.

She sighed. "You ready to go, or what?"

"Prob'ly wants to be a doctor," he said as they went outside, "right?"

"He's majoring in economics."

" 'Scuse *me*," Derek said.

She stopped walking. "A, he's not interested in *me*; B, I'm not interested in *him*, okay?"

He shrugged. "D'I say you were?"

"Everything *but*."

They turned onto Commonwealth Avenue.

"Was work fun?" he asked.

"It was okay. What about you?"

He shrugged. "I was mostly just talking to girls."

"Give it a rest, Derek."

"Are you jealous?"

"I'm *annoyed*," she said.

"Would you be jealous if a girl you didn't know was talking about seeing me on Saturday?"

"Yes. Okay?"

He smiled. "Yeah."

"Are you going to do that every time you come by there?"

"If guys're talking to you, yeah."

"I can't wait," she said.

"Guess it's because, you know, of you being so beautiful and all."

"What does the expression 'pushing your luck' mean to you, Derek?"

He grinned. "We going to do something fun tonight?"

"Sure." They were at her apartment now, and she sat on the front steps. "Like what?"

"Would a movie make you happy?"

She shrugged agreeably. "I have to go running first though."

"I'll come over around nine then?"

She nodded. "What do your parents think about you never being home?"

"My father says, 'Hope you're not slacking off at work, mooning around all day,' and my mother says, 'Look how happy he is, Paul. Leave him alone.' And then, she fixes me a little snack."

"She must spend most of her time fixing you little snacks."

221

"Kind of a lot, yeah," he agreed. "Maybe sometime you'll meet them maybe?"

She nodded, the thought making her nervous already.

"Not like, tomorrow. Just sometime." He bent over her. "Do I get to give you a little kiss?"

She nodded, still shy about that aspect of the whole thing.

He leaned over, giving her a tiny, quick, little kiss.

"That *was* a little one," she said.

He shrugged. "All I asked for."

"Was it all you *wanted*?"

"No," he said, patted her hair, and straightened up. "See you."

She nodded.

Derek was definitely a fixture. Even *more* of a fixture. Like she would come into the apartment after running and find him sitting in the kitchen with Irving and Zoe while Maryanne was upstairs giving Oliver — all muddy from the garden — a bath. Or her father would say, "I'm thinking of getting tickets for the game on Sunday. Should I pick up two extra?" Baseball was actually starting to grow on her, and she could say things like, "Boggs sure had the good stick tonight" and not feel like a jerk.

The job was okay, she even felt like she was sort of making some friends there; Dr. Samuels was okay. Just about everything was on the fairly okay side.

It was July, and she and Derek walked down Charles Street, heading for the movies. He had on a white shirt, which made him look particularly tanned and handsome, and she saw more than one girl check him out as they passed. Actually, a few guys checked him out too, which sort of struck her funny.

"You have a lot of admirers," she said.

"They're looking at *you*."

"Right." She shook her head as he held out his cigarette pack. She was up to two and a half miles a day, and had pretty much decided to make smoking a thing of her past. "Do you purposely buy your shirts a size too small so you can show off your muscles?"

He shrugged. "Keep growing out of them, is all."

"Because of work?"

He shrugged.

"No, seriously. Why *do* you have such a good body?"

"I can make kind of a lovely story about it," he said, flexing his arms.

"Oh, well, go for it."

"Actually, it's a stupid story."

Funny, they were almost starting to talk like each other. "So, tell it anyway."

He shrugged, releasing some smoke. "Well, it's just I was this really twerpy kid when I was thirteen and fourteen and all. Got tall all at once, but I weighed about eighty pounds. So I was always eating like crazy, but I never had money, so I just ripped places off. So like, one day, I rob practically half of Star Market, and they catch me, right? The guy was going to call the police and all, so I asked him for a job and said I'd work free for a month to work off what I stole, and then he could fire me or whatever he wanted."

"This *is* a lovely story," Beverly said.

"Yeah. A little long maybe."

She nodded.

"So, he let me be a stock boy, and I was such a good little cowboy that he gave me the job for real, and even paid me for three of the weeks."

"I'm feeling proud to be an American," Beverly said.

He nodded. "Usually have most people crying by the end. So anyway, I took my first check and bought this set of barbells at Sears. Only," now he grinned, "the sad thing is, I was *such* a twerp, I had to get old Sammy to carry them home for me. He thought it was pretty funny."

"It probably was," Beverly said.

"I didn't think so. Anyway, I practiced every day so I'd get big, and now I even have a bench and everything." He shrugged to indicate the end of the story.

"It's inspirational," she said.

"Be better if I'd had polio or something first."

She laughed.

"What, you don't think so?" He put his hand on her back to steer her across Cambridge Street, then lit another cigarette after carefully stubbing out the other one and throwing it away.

"I wish you wouldn't smoke so much," she said. "It's not good for you."

He shrugged, tossing the package into a trash can.

"That's kind of a waste of money," she said.

He shrugged. "You want me to quit, I'll quit."

"Just like that?"

"Sure," he said. "Always figured if someone asked me to, I would. So — " He shrugged again.

"You really just quit?"

"Yeah." He held out the cigarette in his mouth. "Remind me to *really* enjoy this."

"You'd really quit? Just because I asked you?"

"Well," he looked at her, "always figured it'd depend on who did the asking, you know?"

She blushed.

224

"Better start buying me gum though."

She'd always found gum disgusting. "Can I buy you hard candy instead?"

He sighed deeply. "*All* right." He reached across his body with his free hand. "Will you maybe hold this and like, console me?"

She smiled and took his hand.

" 'Course, it might be easier if you walked on my other side," he said.

"Why don't you walk backwards?" she suggested.

"I'm kind of too cool for that sort of thing."

She sighed deeply, but moved to his other side, taking his hand back. "You could have switched your *cigarette* to your other hand."

"It's my last one — I want to smoke it right-handed."

"Enjoying it?"

"Oh, yeah," he said, and blew a smoke ring.

At the movie theater, they bought tickets to some sequel or other, then stood on line to wait.

"So," he slung his arm around her shoulders, "you looking forward to this?"

"Well, I hated the first one," she said, "but — "

"Shit, really?"

She laughed. "No."

"I mean, if you want, we could — "

"Derek, really," she said. "I'll just suf — " She stopped.

"What's wrong?"

"Nothing," she said quickly. Susan McAllister and Patrick Finnegan were heading toward them, obviously planning to go to the same — she turned the other way, but Susan had already seen her, stopping a few feet away. Patrick also noticed, and his arm protectively circled Susan's waist.

225

They all stared at each other, no one speaking. Then, Susan turned and hurried across the parking lot, almost running. Patrick hesitated, maybe about to say something, but then went after her.

Beverly let out her breath, sinking against the cement wall of the building.

"Kind of think I know who that was," Derek said.

She nodded, her eyes closed.

"You okay?"

"Do you mind if we leave? I'll pay you back."

"Oh, hell, don't worry about *that*." He stepped out of line, intercepting a boy and a girl who had nervous "this is our first date" expressions. "Yo, must be your lucky day," he said, handed them the two movie tickets, and took Beverly's hand.

"I'm sorry," she said. "I didn't mean to — "

He leaned over to kiss the side of her head. "Don't worry about it. There anyplace you want to go?"

She shook her head. "I'm sorry."

"Like I said, no problem."

She didn't want to walk down crowded, brightly lit Charles Street, so they walked on the flat of the Hill instead.

"Doesn't hate you as much as you think she does," he said.

"Yes, she does."

He shook his head. "Could tell by looking at her. Looked *scared* more'n anything else."

"Of *me?*"

"I don't know." He looked over. "Bound to happen someday. Boston's that kind of place."

"Yeah, but I know she lives on Beacon Hill. I should have known better than — "

"Could've happened anywhere," he said. "There's only like, so many movies."

They emerged across from the Public Gardens.

"We could go in there and sit down," he said.

She shrugged, letting him take her over there, and they sat by the water, under a willow tree.

"See that duck?" he said, pointing. "I *know* that duck."

She tried to smile.

"Might be, you'd rather hear about it another time." He patted his pocket, looking for his cigarettes, then remembered and lowered his hand.

"I'm sorry," she said. "I didn't mean to ask you to quit."

"I forgot, is all." He put his arm around her. "You want to talk, or not talk?"

"I don't know." She leaned against him, feeling very tired. "I'm sorry."

" 'Cause we *ran* into someone?" he said. "Hell, worry about *real* stuff."

They sat there, watching the duck swim over to some other ducks.

"I lied," he said suddenly.

She looked up, surprised, the word sounding very strange coming from him.

" 'Bout the barbells," he said.

She waited for him to go on.

"See, my father used to kind of beat up on Sammy, and I figured — well, Sammy was joining up, so I was afraid — seemed like he might be going to start up on me, and — shit." He bent down, picking up a small rock and tossing it into the water.

She didn't know what to say, so she just waited.

"I mean like, I would never hit him back or anything because I totally don't believe in that, but I was thinking — well, I'd like, leave my door open and lift weights and just like, look at him. Didn't seem as bad as saying — " He stopped, looking for another rock. "Kind of pathetic, hunh?"

"Kind of *brave*," she said.

He shrugged, flipping a stick into the water.

"Um, has he ever — ?"

"No," Derek said, and sort of smiled. "Try not to give him a reason."

They looked at each other, Beverly lightly touching his cheek.

"Anyway," Derek said, "he doesn't do it anymore. So — " He shrugged.

"I guess *everyone* has kind of a tough time," she said.

"Yeah. Sometimes." He straightened his cap. "So. How about I walk you home?"

"Unless you'd rather — "

"What the hell," he said, and looked at his watch. "Can catch the last few innings."

"Sounds nice," she said.

Chapter
Twenty-Four

It was hard to sleep that night and she went down to the living room, sitting in the dark to think.

She didn't hear her father until he was passing the couch, and they both jumped, her father maybe even more startled than she was.

"I thought you were asleep," he said.

"I thought all of *you* were."

"I just came down to get something to drink." He paused. "Everything all right?"

She shrugged.

"Well," he said, uncomfortably, and headed for the kitchen.

"I ran into Susan McAllister tonight," she said.

He stopped. "That was unfortunate."

"Yeah."

"Did you — speak?"

"No."

He nodded.

"I wish she knew how sorry I am."

He looked even more uncomfortable.

"Do *you* know how sorry I am?" she asked.

He nodded.

"I really hate it," she said. "I hate all of it. And I'm trying to be different."

"Your — Maryanne and I noticed," he said.

"I'm trying to be different to *her*."

He nodded.

"I guess you're looking forward to August thirty-first." Which was the day she had to be at Wesleyan for orientation.

"In all honesty," he said, "this summer hasn't been quite what I anticipated."

"Is that good?"

He nodded.

"I *am* sorry," she said. "I really am."

"I should have done more to help you," he said. "A number of years ago, I mean."

She shrugged.

"I'm not — inherently parental, shall we say."

She didn't want to agree, so she didn't say anything.

"It's not a case of my not wanting to, just — " He sighed. "I've learned a great deal from Maryanne."

"Does that mean you hate Mom?"

He folded his arms, not looking at her. "I wasn't any better with her than I've been with you."

"Do you think about her?"

He nodded. "Often."

"Do you feel bad?"

"I married your mother because I loved her," he said. "No matter how difficult things get, that doesn't completely go away."

She nodded.

"I wasn't — supportive," he said. "At the time, I don't think I realized the *degree* to which I wasn't, but I very definitely wasn't."

"Did you know it was going to happen?"

He shook his head. "I was aware that her problem with alcohol was increasingly serious, but — "

"She was *sad*," Beverly said.

"I know," he said. "I wish I had realized *how* sad."

"Is that *my* fault?"

"No. I was probably the closest adult to the situation, and — I should have been more aware."

She couldn't think of anything to say and bent to pat Jason, who had wandered downstairs, presumably after her father.

"As upset with you as I've been over the past year, Beverly, I've never been able to forget my own part in the whole thing."

She looked up from Jason. "What do you mean?"

"The fact that you turned to someone like him is quite an indication of what you *weren't* receiving here."

"I really thought he loved me," she said. "And I *did* love him."

Her father nodded.

"You trust Derek, right?"

"Implicitly," her father said.

Saturday at Steve's was very busy and — unfortunately — very short-handed.

"And honey vanilla with M&M's and walnuts," the person she was waiting on said, the end of a long order.

She nodded, bending into the ice cream case. Honey vanilla and Oreo were hard as rocks today.

Hank was next to her, doing something with carob.

231

"What's the deal with the guy in the baseball cap?" he asked.

"Well," she worked on the edge of the ice cream, prying it away from the side of the metal container, "he likes the Red Sox."

"I mean — here" — he reached over — "let me loosen that for you."

Rather than argue, she stepped back.

"I just meant," he was having almost as much trouble digging it out as she had been, "if I asked you out, would you say no?"

"What?" She realized that the customers were listening, which was either funny or embarrassing. Funny for *them*, anyway. "Oh, thank you," she said, as he scooped the appropriate amount of ice cream out onto the counter for her.

He went back to the carob. "So would you?"

She used the little ice cream shovel to make a well in her honey vanilla, dropping in small scoops of M&M's and walnuts, then mashing it all together. Disgusting, really. "As friends, sure."

"Oh, so you guys are pretty serious."

"Well — yeah."

He shrugged. "Oh, well, no harm in asking."

Some good, even. "No harm at all," she agreed, and handed the customer her honey vanilla.

That night — after the game — she and Derek ended up walking down to the Public Gardens to sit on a bench and look at the swan pond.

"You want a little nature lesson?" he asked.

She laughed. "No."

"I give a really nice talk on the life cycle of the moth."

"It *sounds* nice."

"It is." He picked up a stick, then took out his Swiss Army knife. "You want me to make you a little something?"

"Can you do a Ferrari?"

He looked at her, sighed deeply, and threw the stick into the water, several ducks paddling over to examine it.

"Maybe you had something else in mind," she said.

"Maybe," he said, and took out some hard candy, offering her a piece.

"That guy at work, Hank, asked me out."

"Oh." His expression changed, but not enough to classify. Emptied, sort of. "Well, hope you said yes."

"Why do you hope *that*?"

"Be good for you," he said. "Going out with some smart college guy and all."

"He wanted to know if it was serious with that guy in the baseball hat and I said yeah, it is."

"Am I the guy in the baseball hat?"

Instead of answering, she took his cap off, putting it on *her* head.

"Seems like it's something we have to talk about," he said, his expression still blank. "What happens when you leave and all."

"What do you *want* to have happen?"

"I don't know." He threw another stick. "When you leaving?"

"Orientation starts on the thirty-first."

He nodded.

"Derek — "

"Hey, it's good," he said. "You'll meet people more your type." He smiled slightly. "People who write poetry and all."

233

"*You're* my best friend."

"Well, maybe," he said. "But you're going to be like, totally different after you've been there for a while."

"No, I — "

"Nothing wrong with it," he said. "You *should* change when you go away."

"Just because I'm going away doesn't mean — "

"Oh, right," he said. "I'd fit in real well coming to visit and all. Me and all those guys with glasses and alligator shirts. Bet we'll all party down, hunh?"

"Derek, I've never seen you *not* fit in."

He shrugged. "Even if I did, that doesn't mean *we* would anymore. You're going to meet some guy who quotes Shakespeare, and gives a damn about — I don't know — OPEC, and — " He shrugged again.

"That's not going to happen," she said.

"Be realistic," he said. "You're going to be down there getting even smarter and stuff, and *I'm* going to be — "

Losing patience, she punched him in the arm.

"Ow," he said. "Why'd you do that?"

"I don't know." She smiled as he gripped the arm as though he were in pain. "I guess because I love you or something."

He stopped gripping. "What?"

"I know you heard me."

"I don't think I heard *right*."

"I said I *love* you. Okay?"

To her amazement, he blushed. "For real? I mean, you're not just — "

"Derek, how likely is it that I would 'just say' something like that?"

"Well — " He grinned. "Kind of not at all. But, is

234

it just like, as friends and stuff, or — "

Now, *she* blushed. "Not just as friends and stuff."

"Does that mean" — he didn't quite look at her — "I can *really* kiss you? Like, whenever I want?"

"Yeah." She laughed. "I guess that's what it means."

He glanced around the park, which was pretty quiet. "Is now an okay time?"

"Yeah," she said. "Now's great."

Chapter
Twenty-Five

Going to her next-to-last appointment with Dr. Samuels, she felt almost nostalgic. He was a nice man.

"I guess next week will be the last time you'll be seeing me for a while," he said.

She nodded.

"Feel pretty good about that?"

"Well, I called your wife and gave her phone numbers where she can reach me twenty-four hours a day," she said.

He smiled, breaking a bran muffin in half, and she watched him eating it.

"I guess I didn't do a very good job here," she said.

"Oh, I don't know. I thought it was pretty good," he said.

"But — I mean, I didn't cry, or have sex dreams, or anything like that."

"We still have a week to go," he said.

She laughed. "Yeah, well, you just keep hoping." She sat back, looking around the office. Flowers, as always, on the coffee table, and in the little vase on his desk. "Nothing personal," she said, "but I'm still a little worried about you having all these flowers around."

"I like flowers," he said.

"Derek does too. He said that usually city workers move around, but they keep him in the Public Gardens because of his 'like, aesthetics.' " She looked away from the daisies. "Doesn't it get expensive, buying new ones all the time?"

"We have a garden," he said.

"Oh." She adjusted her image of his little bespectacled, curly-brown-haired family. "Where on Long Island did you say you're from?"

"I didn't, but, Syosset."

She grinned. Could she call them, or what? "So, um, did I like, move into the rewarding category?"

"Just about a bull's-eye," he said.

She thought about that. "Derek says you have to have had polio or something to make things *really* good."

Dr. Samuels laughed.

"Do I come back here at Christmas and all?"

"Only if you want to for any reason," he said.

"Does that mean you think I'll *need* to?"

"No. But I wouldn't mind hearing how you're doing."

She nodded.

"Are you looking forward to school?"

"I don't know. I mean, I'm scared, but it's probably normal scared." She stretched a little, her muscles cramping from sitting still. "Did I tell you I got a letter from my roommate?"

He shook his head.

"My father says she 'sounds like a lovely young girl.' "

Dr. Samuels grinned.

"She — well, she has hobbies."

"Oh, boy," Dr. Samuels said.

"Yeah," she agreed. "But, I don't know. I'm not exactly a door prize myself."

"You're not so bad."

"Well, it's not like I have to tell everyone my whole damned life story, right?" she said.

"As long as it doesn't fester."

She nodded, and it was quiet.

"I don't want to leave Derek either," she said.

"That sounds normal too."

She nodded.

"Do you feel you've accomplished anything by coming here?"

"I don't know," she said. "Did I tell you I can run three-and-a-half miles now?"

"That's pretty good," he said, in the voice of a man who did a push-up every six months.

"I'm going to stop at four. After that — I don't know — it seems like they turn into zealots."

He nodded.

"When I wake up in the morning now, I don't think about killing myself."

"What *do* you think about?"

"I don't know." She considered that. "Derek. If I'm late for work. If we're out of Cap'n Crunch."

He nodded.

"Derek."

He nodded again.

"I don't know."

It was quiet.

"So," she said, but in a friendly voice. "Is it time for me to leave yet, or what?"

He grinned. "Almost."

Derek was pretty tired that night, so they just talked on the phone, and then she watched television with Oliver. When it was over, and Maryanne was putting him to bed, she went up to her room, sitting down at her desk. She looked down at her bottom desk drawer, deciding that she might as well open it. See if it was still Pandora's Box.

It was still mostly pictures. She spread a batch out across her desk, studying them. A picture of her, maybe four years old, in the shallow end of some motel pool, wearing tiny red sunglasses. A picture of her, maybe a year older, looking less than excited by a playground swing. A picture of her with her mother, opening a window on the advent calendar. Oh, hell.

She sat back, looking at the ceiling. Christmas. She really ought to yank out all the stupid Christmas pictures. She lifted a picture at random, looking at it. Her sitting at the kitchen table in Hanover, with her friend Tracy Grossman, her tongue caught between her teeth as they worked intently on a batch of cookies. That's right, her mother was always having them bake cookies. Oh, hell.

"Beverly, I — " Maryanne stopped in the doorway. "I'm sorry, I thought because the door was open — "

Beverly put the picture down. "It's okay."

"Well, I just — you don't have that much time, and I thought you might want to make a list of things you're going to need for school."

"Okay."

"I mean, things like hangers, and extension cords,

239

and — " Maryanne stopped. "But you said okay, didn't you."

Beverly nodded.

"I'm sorry, I hope I didn't disturb you." Maryanne said, leaving.

"Do you want to look at some pictures?"

Her stepmother turned.

"I was just — well, looking at some."

"Do you *want* me to?" her stepmother asked.

"Sure. I mean, as long as *you* want to."

Maryanne came in, sitting down on the edge of the bed. She was wearing jeans — big surprise — and an old New England Patriots shirt, the sleeves pushed way up. It looked almost stylish.

Beverly handed her a picture. "This is me, going to kindergarten."

Maryanne smiled. "*Partridge Family* lunchbox."

"I was pretty hip." Beverly smiled at the picture herself. "After that, I had a *Charlie's Angels* one." She picked up another photograph, one of her — quite small — in front of the Fenway Park box seats entrance, wearing a little cap and holding a Red Sox pennant. Her father had a cap on, too. "This was one time when we drove down for a game. I think it might have been the year they went to the World Series."

"You and Oliver have the same smile," Maryanne said.

Beverly nodded. "Kind of." She looked at the picture. "I have a damned pointy chin."

Maryanne grinned. "Kind of."

Beverly picked up another — her mother on her birthday, while Beverly stood next to her, peering up at the cake her grandmother was holding. There were a few others with it — her mother opening various presents, trying on her new skirt, standing with her father. She hesitated, but handed them to Maryanne. "I guess my grandmother was first getting sick right around then," she said.

Maryanne nodded, looking at the pictures, her hair falling forward across part of her face.

There were more pictures, but Beverly only lifted a few out of the drawer. "Funny," she said, looking at one of her standing in front of the Dartmouth Political Science building with her father. "She almost always took them, instead of being in them. I wish — well." She gave that one to Maryanne, coming across a few of the various sights of Dartmouth Winter Carnival. She was usually in them — wearing a bulky blue ski jacket and her matching red plaid hat and scarf set, standing in front of snow and ice sculptures.

She pulled out another one — of her, smiling happily after her first-grade play, still wearing her Pilgrim costume, her mother behind her with her arms around her, looking so proud — so damn — she let out her breath. "Oh, God." She looked at the picture, feeling a deep pain in her stomach that wasn't anything like the ulcer. Remembering Maryanne next to her, she let out another shaky breath. "I — do you feel like looking at any more of these?"

Maryanne shook her head.

"Good." Beverly gathered the pictures up, very neatly, replacing them in the drawer. "I — I guess you can overdose on them." She started to close the drawer, lifted out her mother's watch, then closed it completely. "Samuels says I ought to wear one of these, instead of bugging people about what time it is all the time."

Maryanne nodded.

"I probably will," she said, putting the watch in her pocket. She looked up. "Glad you came in here?"

Maryanne reached over to touch her shoulder and for once, Beverly didn't jerk away. She looked around the room, touching the watch in her pocket.

"You know," she said finally. "I hate what happened to my family, but — " She sighed. "If I didn't know you and Oliver, I'd be sad."

Her stepmother almost seemed to hold her breath. "You don't have to say that."

Beverly grinned. "You're right. I don't."

Chapter
Twenty-Six

It was Monday, and — not surprisingly — Derek showed up near the end of her shift at Steve's.

"Can I kiss you," he asked, his voice extra-loud so her manager would hear, "or will your buddy Bill get upset?"

"Bill will get upset," her manager said, checking stock below the counter.

"Well, then, guess I'd better just have a milkshake." He pointed at the carob. "Make it quick, miss."

Beverly grinned wryly and started scooping. "Shouldn't you be at work?"

"Quit my job," he said, very cheerful.

She stopped scooping. "What?"

"Gave my notice a couple of weeks ago, actually."

"Why didn't you tell me?"

"Wanted to see what happened after," he said. "I mean, before I told you."

"You're not — " She lowered her voice. "I mean, before you said you might join the Army."

"Yeah." Now, he grinned. "Got another job today, *actually.*"

She put the metal cup on the milkshake mixer without really looking at it. "Doing what?"

"Well — you're about to make an ugly mess."

She saw that she'd put the cup on crooked, and that it was about to spray ice cream all over the place. She straightened it. "Doing what?"

"Saw an ad for a carpenter's apprentice and" — his grin widened — "son of a bitch if they didn't hire me."

"Hey, that's great," she said. "I mean, you love wood."

"Well, yeah, that's what I was telling them."

"Wow." She nodded. "That's really great."

"Yeah," he said. "They're pretty cool guys. I mean," he winked at her, "a couple of them went to Harvard, so I don't know, but — "

"My father will be pleased," she said.

"Yeah, I figured," he said. "It's out like, near Somerville, so I'll probably end up getting an apartment out there." He glanced at her.

"Sounds good," she said, making sure that no one else overheard her.

"Did to me too."

When the milkshake was ready, he took it over to a table, sitting down to wait for her. There were only a few customers, and she checked her mother's watch to see how much time she had left.

She was making a hot fudge sundae when she saw Susan McAllister coming in, and froze. Should she go into the back room, or just stall until someone else waited on her, or — Susan had recognized Derek and nodded at him before coming up to the front.

"Hi," she said.

"Uh, hi," Beverly said, spraying whipped cream so she wouldn't have to look all the way up.

"Your friend seems to be making his move to Canada Dry," Susan said, indicating Derek, and Beverly almost smiled, knowing without looking that he was sitting there singing to himself. "Your, uh, your stepmother said you got off pretty soon."

Beverly nodded, handing the sundae to the woman who'd ordered it.

"Do you have plans with him?"

"Not really."

"Is it okay if I wait around?"

"Uh, sure. Um" — Beverly indicated the order board — "do you want anything?"

Susan shook her head. "No, thanks." She sat down at a table by the window and Beverly rang up the sale, seeing Derek pick up his milkshake, go over and sit across from her.

"You've got friends waiting," Bill said from behind her. "Why don't you take off a little early?"

Friends? "Oh, no, I don't have to — "

"I think we'll survive," he said. "Just fill up the Heath Bars and the raisins, and you can leave."

"Okay," she said. "I mean, thank you." She glanced out front, seeing Derek and Susan deep in conversation. She filled the containers, then slowly untied her apron, going to the back room to wash her hands and punch out. When she came out, Derek stood up, tipped his baseball cap at her, and left. Even more uneasy, she walked over to the table.

"He said he'd 'catch you later,' " Susan said.

Beverly nodded, folding her arms.

"He's very nice."

Beverly nodded.

"I, uh — " Susan's smile was weak. "I'm not sure why I'm here."

"When do you leave for school?"

"Friday."

Beverly nodded. She was leaving on Saturday.

"Hey, Beverly," Hank said, coming in for his shift, and she nodded at him, too nervous to say anything back.

"You look different," Susan said. "Healthier."

Beverly grinned sheepishly. "I started running."

"How far do you go?"

"Not very."

Susan nodded.

"Uh, what kind of summer did you have?"

"Quiet." Susan smiled a little. "Therapeutic."

Beverly nodded, knowing what *that* meant.

"Does it, um, seem noisy in here?" Susan asked, indicating the tables.

"Maybe we should walk around?"

Susan nodded, and they went outside. As they walked, Beverly noticed that she was both taller and a lot more relaxed than Susan was. And this was the person she was *afraid* of? Someone who looked like a nice, nervous kid her age? It seemed strange now.

They ended up sitting on a bench on Commonwealth Avenue.

"I was really a jerk at the movies that time," Susan said. "I guess I panicked, I don't know."

Beverly nodded. "I didn't expect you to be there that night," she said, after a pause. "At his house, I mean. I mean, when I *saw* you, I — " She shook her head. "I guess I thought you'd be at the hospital. Because of Patrick and all."

"I *was*," Susan said. "I just. . . . I thought I had to get proof. That he might — confess or something."

Beverly nodded.

"I spent a lot of time thinking terrible things about you," Susan said. "All kinds of 'what if's.' "

"Like," Beverly said, "what if he had killed me instead of just beating me up, and been put away almost a year earlier."

Susan flushed guiltily.

"Why not me — especially since I didn't seem to want to be around — instead of Colleen."

Susan's nod was embarrassed. "I'm sorry."

"You're sorry?" Beverly pressed her fist down on her knee, noticing how tanned her hand was. She *did* look healthy. "I wished the same thing — probably harder than you did. I mean, Christ, you wouldn't be normal if you didn't — " She hesitated, but went on. "He killed your best friend."

Susan looked at her. "People usually don't put it that bluntly."

"I'm sorry."

"No. It *is* that blunt." Susan swallowed. "He killed my best friend." Her eyes brightened and she looked away, her hand coming up to cover them. "I keep thinking it's going to get easier," she said shakily.

"It does."

Susan glanced over, her eyes so full of tears that blinking would be enough to knock them out.

"It does," Beverly said, more quietly. "Before, I cried when I heard anything about mothers. Or families, or — it seemed like everything set me off."

247

"How long did it take?"

Beverly sighed. "Pretty long. And it comes back." She hesitated. "Does Patrick help?"

"He tries," Susan said, "but — well, he's having a pretty hard time too." She wiped her hand across her eyes, then looked over. "Could you have prevented it?"

Beverly didn't answer right away. "I don't think so," she said. "I mean, I could tell he was getting scared, but I never thought — I mean, I guess I thought the worst he would do was scare her. Because she was a girl, and he thought girls — Jesus, I don't know. I was just too scared."

Susan nodded. "Were you friends with her?" she asked.

"No. But I liked her."

Susan slouched forward, her hands covering most of her face. "She'd hate this — me being so upset and everything. Probably say, 'The Queen is dead, long live the Queen' and all of that."

Beverly had to smile. "She *would* say that."

Susan smiled too. "Yeah." The smile left. "You know, that was supposed to be my first day of school here. Why she couldn't wait *two* hours for me to be — " The smile came back, feebly. "Stupid to be mad at her, on top of everything else.

"*He's* the son of a bitch who deserves it."

"Yeah." Susan closed her eyes, taking in and releasing a deep breath. "You have to be at the trial, right?"

Beverly nodded.

"Could we try to be friends? So it would be easier?"

Beverly nodded.

"Good." Susan looked at her for a minute. "You

248

know, you're the only other one who's ever *really* going to understand it. Understand *him*, especially."

Beverly nodded.

"It still seems so — I mean, I think about it, and I can't believe — " Susan laughed, sounding very close to tears. "I miss her so much."

"I'm sorry," Beverly said. "I mean, I'm *really* sorry."

Susan nodded. "I know you are. Thank you." Abruptly, she stood up. "I'd better go — I told my parents I was just going for a little walk."

Beverly nodded, also standing.

They looked at each other for a minute.

"Good luck at school," Beverly said.

"Yeah, you too," Susan said, then sighed. "You too."

She was only a couple of blocks away from home, but Beverly found walking them very tiring. As she turned onto Marlborough Street, she saw Derek sitting on her front steps.

"Hi," he said.

"Hi." She stopped at the bottom of the steps, not having enough energy to go up them. "A hug might be sort of swell."

He grinned, coming down to hug her, Beverly hugging back.

"Thank you," she said, her face against his chest.

"No, see, you don't get it," he said. "I enjoy this too."

"I meant, just in general. For — I don't know — existing, I guess."

"Pretty intense," he said.

"Yeah." She kissed him, hard, then stepped back. "Will you stay for dinner maybe?"

He grinned. "Your father already asked me."

249

"Figures," she said.

"And can we maybe watch the game after?"

"I don't know," she said. "Can I wear your hat?"

"Seems to me like you ought to get your *own* hat."

"I want to wear *yours*."

"Well, I don't know." He sighed deeply. "Would it make you happy?"

She grinned, putting it on. "Yeah," she said. "It would make me happy."

About the Author

ELLEN EMERSON WHITE's favorite joke is: If I dialed the wrong number, why did you answer the phone? She is the author of several books for young adults, among them *The President's Daughter, White House Autumn,* and *Friends for Life,* which is a companion book to *Life Without Friends.*

Ellen Emerson White grew up in Narragansett, Rhode Island, and was graduated from Tufts University in 1983. She now works full-time as a writer, and lives in Boston.